$\mathcal{I}$ rolled over and sighed. It was still dark and dreary, but my internal clock told me I needed coffee.

Wearing my not-so-sexy flannel trousers and long-sleeved shirt, I clambered out of bed and put on my fuzzy purple slippers. Shivering, I slipped on my thick robe, but didn't bother to tie it. I was going to head quickly down the stairs to the bathroom, where hopefully I could find more warmth, along with my toothbrush and hairbrush.

I dashed down the narrow steps. When I got to the bottom of the stairs, I turned into the hallway and came up short.

A lumberjack was standing there.

Or at least that's what he looked like. A really young, really *hot* lumberjack. He was tall and broad, with midnight black hair that curled around his ears and across his brow, creating the perfect frame for his startling blue eyes.

He grinned. "Hey."

Also by Rachel Hawthorne

Snowed In

RACHEL HAWTHORNE

HARPER TEEN
An Imprint of HarperCollins*Publishers*

HarperTeen is an imprint of HarperCollins Publishers.

Snowed In
Copyright © 2008 by Rachel Hawthorne

Library of Congress catalog card number: 2007933637
ISBN 978-0-06-113836-2

❖

First Edition

For Amber Royer,
librarian extraordinaire,
who convinced me
this story needed bats

1

"It'll be fun!"

Those were my mom's words. *It'll be fun!*

At the time, I'd thought so too.

Her idea of fun was to pack up her divorced middle-aged life and move up north. Way up north. Where winters are cold, snow and ice exist in abundance, and my dad could become a distant memory.

Not that I blamed her for wanting to get away from it all. Dad recently announced that he planned to remarry, and I'm not exactly thrilled with the prospect of having a stepmother. Marsha isn't wicked or anything. Actually she asked me to be one of her bridesmaids, but I told her that I needed to think about it. I've never been a bridesmaid before, and I'm not sure I want my first time to be at my dad's wedding. Because it's totally weird thinking of him with a wife who isn't my mom. And okay, I resent that he's going to marry someone else. It feels like he's not only betraying Mom, but betraying me.

So when Mom told me she wanted to move and asked, "What do you think?" I replied, "Let's do it!"

Of course, that was before I was standing in the front parlor of our new digs, shivering, with my parka zipped up tightly and my gloved hands tucked beneath my arms, searching for a little extra warmth.

It was, like, negative one thousand degrees outside. You think I'm exaggerating, but Mom's idea of fun included moving to an island on the Great Lakes—in the middle of *winter*, when the surrounding water was starting to freeze. It was that cold. Although cold doesn't adequately describe it. It was much, much colder than cold.

I was going to have to pull out my thesaurus and learn a whole list of adjectives for *cold*.

We'd flown into the small airport about an hour earlier. Our luggage had been loaded onto a taxi, only this taxi was a wagon with runners instead of wheels, because, oh, yeah, the island is covered in mounds of white glistening snow.

I'd actually been excited when Mom mentioned the snow, because arcticlike weather was a totally new experience for me. I've spent most of my seventeen years living in north Texas. When it snows half an inch, schools and businesses shut down, and the local news interrupts the regularly scheduled programming to provide up-to-the-minute progress reports on the trucks dumping sand on the expressways. The reporters stand on overpasses explaining that it's *really* cold, while showing footage of fishtailing vehicles, people slipping (yes, falling down on icy streets is newsworthy in north Texas), and children sliding down hills on baking sheets because we don't, as a rule, invest money in sleds.

I'm pretty certain that kids here have sleds, and that the news isn't going to include roving reporters asking people how they'll deal with the half inch of snow forecast to arrive by nightfall. Here snow is measured in feet—possibly yards—and freezing is clearly a way of life.

Cars, motorcycles, and trucks aren't, however.

Did I forget to mention that? The island has a ban on motorized vehicles. They're left on the mainland.

Mom thinks this is "quaint."

I haven't quite decided, although I'm trying to be open-minded about it. I was hoping to guilt Dad into buying me a red Ford Mustang when I graduate from high school. So I either need to guilt him into buying me something else, be content to drive only occasionally when I'm on the mainland, or move off the island permanently. Something to think about later. Right now, I was suffering from brain freeze.

"There, I think I can feel warm air blowing out now," Mom said. She was standing on a chair, her one bare hand—the other was still gloved—pressed against a vent in the ceiling.

She'd adjusted the thermostat on the heater as soon as we walked through the door. Then she'd lit a fire in the gas fireplace in the parlor. I discovered that a gas-burning fire with fake logs doesn't generate as much heat as a wood-burning one. But then it's not as much trouble to start and keep going, either.

Mom stepped off the chair, faced me, and grinned. But it wasn't her natural grin. It looked fake, painted on, forced, as though she didn't want to acknowledge that we'd made a huge mistake. My mom is the most honest person I know, but this smile had the makings of a con—like the one you get when your mom takes you to the doctor and tells you that whatever the doctor is going to do, it won't hurt. But it does—always. And so you start to recognize that smile and dread it.

Mom removed her woolen cap and static electricity made her short blond hair stick up at various angles. I figured my own blond hair—which hangs just past my chin and, under normal circumstances, which these were not, curls at the ends—would do the same thing when I removed my cap. But I'd read somewhere that a huge amount of body heat escapes through the head, so I kept my hat snugly in place, trying to trap as much heat as possible inside my five-foot-two-inch frame.

"It just takes the air a while to warm up, which makes sense if you think about it, since the air is so cold," Mom said, rambling, as though trying to convince herself as well as me that everything was going to be all right.

"And once it gets warm, it'll stay warm," I said optimistically.

"Oh, definitely," Mom said, her fake smile shifting into a more normal-looking one. "I doubt we'll ever turn off the heater."

"Except during the summer."

"Maybe not even then. Depends on whether or not we've thawed out." She laughed. "Who would have thought cold could be this cold?"

"It's an excuse to buy more clothes."

"Like you need an excuse," Mom said.

Okay, I was a clothesaholic. I loved buying

clothes. I was pretty pumped that I was going to need to stock up on winter clothes that I'd never needed to buy before.

Mom spread her arms wide. "Welcome to Chateau Ashleigh. Our new home and business."

I smiled at that pronouncement. Couldn't help myself. She'd named our new Victorian bed-and-breakfast after me: Ashleigh Sneaux—pronounced *Snow*. In our present circumstances, the irony of that didn't escape me.

Mom had kept the name a secret, so when we arrived, I was totally stunned to see the carved wooden sign hanging on a post near the white picket fence surrounding the Victorian house. It's so like Mom to do something special for me, and I have to admit that I think the name sounds a bit romantic, which would go with Mom's goal to create a romantic atmosphere for guests.

Mom's a romantic at heart, in spite of the fact that things for her and Dad didn't last forever. I admire that about her—that she isn't bitter about being part of a statistic. She still wants to go in search of better things, something she didn't have a chance to do when she was younger, since she and Dad got married the summer after they graduated from high school.

Mom's always advising me to wait. "Have fun,

enjoy life, get married later, much, much later."

Not a problem. Quite honestly, I wasn't even interested in having a boyfriend. I know that sounds strange. Every girl I knew was obsessed with having a steady guy. Not me. I was, however, obsessed with guys—plural. I liked dating guys. Lots of guys. For short periods of time. It's sorta like going to a wine tasting, I guess, where you taste samples of wine until you find one that you really like. Then you buy it in abundance. Not that I've ever been to a wine tasting, but I've heard things.

Anyway, that was sorta my attitude when it came to guys. Try them all. Don't settle, because as soon as you do, someone else might come along and then you have to go through the whole breakup thing before you can go out with him. Better to keep the options open. Besides, there are a lot of guys to sample!

Or at least there were back home. I'd dated several guys at my school, and I was all about exploring possibilities.

Here the possibilities would be severely limited. The island has one school, grades kindergarten through twelfth. The junior class has five students—six when I enroll after the winter break. So getting married is definitely not in my immediate future. As a matter of fact, getting a date might not be doable either. I didn't want to think that I might be reduced to online dating.

Yeah, right. Hook up with a serial killer, why don't you, Ash?

My guilty pleasure is horror movies. The more horrific the better. So I have a tendency to view danger in the world where none exists. I get a rush at the idea of people in peril—in the movies anyway. Someday I want to write a horror novel, and Mom's plan of moving to a small island with a tiny population has called out to the writer in me, the part that craves solitude and quiet in order for the muse to come out and play.

"I'm not planning to make any changes to this room," Mom said suddenly, snapping me away from my thoughts.

Mom's a fixer-upper lover. The previous owners left not only their furniture, but the need for numerous repairs. Hence Mom's reasoning that we needed to move here during the winter—before tourist season—so we could fancy things up and get the business ready to go. I really appreciated that she considered me her business partner.

Of course, I wouldn't get too involved until summer. School comes first, and that works for me. The "bed" part of our B&B means making other people's beds, when I'm not exactly in the habit of making my own. The "breakfast" part means cooking breakfast for strangers. I don't even make breakfast for myself. Nor am I prone to getting up early unless I absolutely have to.

Mom removed her other glove and quickly shoved both hands into the pockets of her parka, unwilling, I guess, to admit that the house still wasn't warm enough. I wondered if it ever would be.

"Ready for the grand tour?" Mom asked.

I smiled. "Sure. Why not?"

She did a Vanna White arm extension, indicating the room in which we were standing. "The parlor, where we'll serve afternoon tea."

A worn Oriental rug covered most of the hardwood flooring. A couch, a couple of chairs, and a coffee table were arranged in front of the fireplace. Other plush armchairs sat in front of the bay window. The curtains were drawn back and the front porch that spanned the width of the house was visible. Someone—a kind neighbor perhaps—had generously shoveled away the snow from the porch, the steps, and the front walk, so Mom and I had been granted safe passage into the house when we'd arrived. I had a feeling that in the days ahead, shoveling snow was going to become one of my jobs. I suddenly found myself wishing that I had a brother.

Half a dozen small dried flower arrangements were scattered throughout the room, on the mantel, on various small tables. Cluttered didn't begin to describe the décor.

Mom led me through the entryway. The front door had an amazing oval-shaped etched-glass window. We walked across the hardwood floor and into the library.

The room smelled musty and ancient. Along two walls, dark bookshelves stretched to the ceiling. Another bay window with the draperies pulled back offered a slightly different view of the outside. I could see the snow-covered lawn and street.

A large desk sat near the window. Everything looked antique. Not a computer in sight.

Mom and I went down the hallway, passing a bathroom on the right, turning into an alcove on our left before we got to the stairs. The alcove led to the dining room.

"We'll serve breakfast in here," Mom said.

A big, sturdy table sat in the center. A china hutch held plates and glasses. Portraits taken about a hundred years ago adorned the walls. I figured they were just to create atmosphere. I mean, if they were portraits of the previous owners' family, surely they would have taken them.

We went through the room and into the kitchen.

"Let me guess," I said. "This is where we'll cook."

Mom laughed. She has a really nice laugh. Soft and full of fun. And she laughed all the time. Or at least she had BD—Before Divorce. As much as I hadn't wanted to leave my friends in Texas, I was hoping that Mom would be happier here and laugh more.

"Don't give me a hard time, Miss Smarty-pants." She walked to the sink and looked out the window at the backyard, which was blanketed in snow.

I remembered reading somewhere that people could go blind—and crazy—surrounded by snow, because all the white is disorienting. I wondered if people got lost here, if they had rescue dogs.

"This is going to be fun," Mom said with a sigh.

"It's really quiet here, though, isn't it," I said, more as a statement than a question.

She turned around. "That's because there aren't any cars."

But still, the silence was eerie. I told myself that it was because I wasn't used to it. But it was more than that.

"It's just so horror movie–ish," I said. "You know. A mother and daughter in an old house that creaks and moans and . . . it's cold. Houses in horror movies are always cold."

Mom shook her head. "I don't know why you like watching scary movies so much."

I joined her at the window. I'd always been fascinated by the idea of snow, but now that I was actually here I found it a bit unsettling. In a few more weeks, the ferry that runs between the island and the mainland would shut down for a couple of months. Then we'd be trapped.

Deranged killers and psychos would have a field day before the first thaw. And no one would know until it was too late. Hadn't I seen that scenario in a movie? I shuddered at the thought.

"So why do you think the owners wanted to sell the place?" I asked.

"Because it's haunted."

2

I felt my eyes widen and my jaw drop. "Seriously?"

Laughing, Mom reached out and snatched off my cap. Yeah, my hair did the whole flying-around-my-head thing. I hadn't considered that living in the cold would mean endless bad hair days.

"No, silly," Mom said. "It's not haunted. The owners wanted to retire. So here we are. Why don't you go pick out your bedroom? Any room you want."

"Which room are you going to take?"

"Back behind the stairs is a large bedroom. I'm going to take that one. I figured you'd want something higher up."

"Definitely."

Back in the hallway, I grabbed my backpack, deciding to leave my suitcase. No sense in lugging it around until I picked which room I wanted.

Most of our stuff was being shipped here. Until it arrived, I had only the essentials of my life.

The doorbell rang, and through the etched glass on the front door, I saw the shadowy outline of two people. I wasn't certain I should open the door. I was pretty sure I wouldn't know them. And what was the crime rate here? Would anyone even hear us scream?

Mom's hurried footsteps echoed between the walls as she rushed from the kitchen. Having removed her parka, she rounded the corner into the hallway. She was wearing a mint green sweater that matched her eyes—and mine. My grandma always told me how much I looked like Mom when she was younger. It gave me hope that I'd look like her when I was older. She was pretty. Another reason I didn't understand Dad wanting to marry someone else.

"Open the door, Ashleigh." But she rushed past me and did what she'd ordered me to do. It was part of her AD (After Divorce) personality. She wanted to control everything.

A girl about my age and a woman a bit older than Mom stood on the porch, their breath coming out in white wisps, their cheeks and noses red from the cold.

"Hello!" the woman exclaimed before Mom

could say anything. "I'm Laura Evans and this is my daughter, Nathalie. We saw you arrive earlier and wanted to welcome you to the neighborhood."

"Come in," Mom said, and then introduced us.

"I brought you some warm spice cake," Mrs. Evans said.

"How sweet," Mom replied. "Would you and Natalie—"

"Not Natalie," Mrs. Evans said. "Nathalie. I didn't know whether to name her after my older brother, Nathan, or my younger brother, Leland, and so I combined the two and made up a name."

"How original," Mom said.

Nathalie and I looked at each other, and clearly neither of us could believe the inane conversation our moms were having. I felt an instant connection with her—and also a sense of relief. Knowing so few kids lived on the island had caused me some apprehension about moving. What if I didn't meet anyone I liked? Would I live here without any dates *or* friends?

Nathalie pushed back the hood of her coat, revealing red hair pulled into a ponytail. If she lived in Texas, she'd have a lot more freckles. Her nose turned up on the end. She was a little taller than I was and quite pretty.

Mom took their coats, which left me feeling a

little ridiculous—I was still bundled up. So I took off mine and helped Mom hang everything in the hall closet.

"Ashleigh, why don't you and Nathalie get settled into the parlor, while Mrs. Evans and I make some tea to go with this wonderful-smelling spice cake?" Mom suggested, before leading Mrs. Evans away.

I looked at Nathalie. She didn't even look cold. I had a feeling that I did. I still couldn't feel my nose.

"You know, if you spray Static Guard on your brush and run it through your hair, it'll make it stop flying around like that," she said, twirling her finger near her hair like she was trying to say I was crazy.

"Thanks for the tip. I have a lot to learn about living in the cold."

"So, where are you guys from?"

"Texas."

"You don't sound like a cowgirl."

"I'm not. I'm a city girl."

"Why did you and your mom move here then?" she asked.

"Mom was looking for something different."

She laughed. "Well, I'm sure you're going to

find it here. Isn't Texas all desert and tumble-weeds?"

Now it was my turn to laugh. "No. Not all of it. We have woods, mountains, hills, lakes, rivers. You name it, we pretty much have it."

"Not according to the movies. You know, they made a movie here once," she said.

"Really?"

"Yeah. They used the ritzy hotel that's up on the hill, just up the road. Women aren't even allowed on the grounds after five o'clock if they're not wearing a dress."

"You're kidding."

She shook her head. "No. Mom says they're very traditional. I think they're dumb."

"Gotta say I agree with you. So do they make a lot of movies here?"

"Only a couple, but a lot of actors come here to get away from it all. I saw Heath Ledger once."

"No way! In person?"

She nodded, then shrugged. "At least, I think it was him. My boyfriend didn't agree."

"You have a boyfriend?"

"Yeah, sure. Don't you?"

"No, not really."

"Why not?"

"I'm not really interested in having a boyfriend."

She looked at me suspiciously. "Why not?"

I shrugged. "Just figure I have plenty of time to get serious later."

"Do you date?"

"Oh, yeah, sure. I really like dating."

"I can't imagine not having a boyfriend."

I smiled. "I can't imagine having one."

She looked at me like I'd come from another planet.

"So, do you want to sit in there?" I pointed to the parlor, realizing I never really imagined I'd ever invite anyone to sit in one. I mean, really, who had parlors these days?

"Not really. I've never been inside this house. The Shoemakers didn't have kids, so . . ." She shrugged as though that explained it all.

The Shoemakers were the previous owners, and I guessed Nathalie was hoping for a tour.

"Today's the first time for me, too," I said. We both laughed. I'd forgotten how hard it was to get to know someone. But Nathalie made it seem easy.

"Where's your bedroom?" she asked.

"I was just about to take a look around and decide. Want to come with me?"

"You betcha. Sure beats having tea with my

mom. Her idea of exciting conversation is discussing Victorian lace."

I grimaced.

She nodded. "Exactly."

As we climbed the worn wooden stairs, each of our steps echoed around us. The house had been built sometime in the 1880's, and it sounded old, felt old. Okay, it felt haunted. The perfect setting for a horror movie.

When we got to the second floor, it was like we'd stepped even further back in time.

A short hallway to my right led to a couple of bedrooms that were separated by a bathroom.

"Oh, totally awesome!" Nathalie said as she peered into one of the rooms. "I think all the furniture is antique. You must have paid a fortune for this."

Mom probably had, but, fortunately, money is one of the things that isn't a problem for us. Dad is a big corporate executive. He and Mom split everything they'd acquired over the years right down the middle. Except for me, of course. If they fought about anything, I didn't know about it. That didn't make it any easier, and I can't deny there were a lot of tears. But at least there wasn't really any bitterness—or financial squabbling.

Nathalie looked at me. "People really get into

the old stuff around here. The Victorian Walk is next weekend. A lot of the houses are opened up for touring, and all the money collected goes to the Historical Preservation Society. I'm selling tickets if you want to go."

Looking through old houses really wasn't my thing, but I was trying to make a friend here and I didn't want to hurt her feelings.

"I might. I don't really know. I mean, I just got here."

"Oh, right. Sorry. Guess you need to find a bedroom before you start planning your social calendar."

Would I even have a social calendar here? Would I meet other kids? Would we hit it off? Would we want to do things together?

"Anyway, I thought you said you'd never been inside this house," I said.

"Right. The Shoemakers usually closed it up and headed to Florida for the winter, so this one was never included on the tour. I'm guessing they decided to sell and stay down there?"

"I think so."

"Fine by me. They were totally no fun."

"Do a lot of people leave for the winter?" I asked.

Nathalie shrugged. "Some do. Most don't.

Most of our businesses rely on tourism, and since we don't get many tourists in winter, some people will close up shop and head to sunnier places." She laughed. "I sound like a Chamber of Commerce ad, don't I?" She peered into another room. "So which one is going to be yours?"

"I don't know."

I went in the other direction, walking along the carpet that lined the floor. Quickly I looked into the four bedrooms on that end of the hallway. The rooms had canopied beds and lots of lace and frills.

I figured this would be a popular floor for our guests, and I was looking for privacy. I'm not unfriendly, but I wasn't sure how much I'd like living with strangers.

At the end of the hallway was another set of stairs.

"I'm going to check out the next floor," I said.

"I'll come with you," she said as she followed me up the stairs.

On the next floor, we went in different directions, looking in the various rooms. "These aren't that much different from the ones on the floor below," Nathalie said. "Is your mom going to let you fix up your room however you want?"

"I hope so."

"Let me know if you want to paint it. My boyfriend and I can help you."

That was *exactly* what I wanted—to be a third wheel.

My best friend, Tara, had recently hooked up with a guy, so I knew from experience that it isn't fun hanging out with someone when the boyfriend's around.

"Thanks, but I'm not sure what I'm going to do yet," I told her.

At the other end of the hallway was yet another set of stairs. They were much narrower than any of the others. And they creaked more. Halfway up was a small circular window that looked out on the frozen land and the surrounding lake. My new home.

The stairs ended. To my left was a door with an ornate glass doorknob that rattled when I turned it. As I opened the door, the hinges squeaked as if they were practicing to be the sound effects in a Hitchcock movie.

Sunlight filtered through the windows, but still the room was a little dim. I glanced around cautiously, looking for spiderwebs, but couldn't see any.

I did see the light switch, though, so I flipped it on. It didn't make a lot of difference. The four bulbs in the tulip-shaped holders in the ceiling must have been about fifteen watts. But they made enough of a difference that I could see I'd discovered my haven.

When Mom and I arrived, I had noticed that one of the upper rooms had a rounded corner, a turret. This was it.

"Totally awesome!" Nathalie said. "I love this room!"

I was pretty crazy about it too. In the curved corner was a small sitting area. One side of the room had a window seat covered in pillows of various shades of pink. Vents along the floor blew in the warm air that had finally started circulating through the house after Mom turned on the heater downstairs. A brass bed with a lacy pink canopy caught my attention. So romantic. On either side of the bed were windows that looked out onto the front lawn, the lake, and the trees with their leafless branches covered in icicles and snow.

"I'll bet this is where a servant slept," she said. "I think they always made them sleep in the attic."

"Is this the attic?" I asked.

Shrugging, she sat on the window seat, brought her feet up to the pillows, and wrapped her arms around her legs. "You have *got* to have a sleepover up here."

I sat on the bed. "Sleepover implies multiple friends."

Her light blue eyes twinkled. "Hey, you've got me. And I have friends."

"How many friends?"

She laughed. "What kind of a question is that?"

"Well, I researched the school . . . and there aren't a lot of kids on the island. Back home, we had more than twelve hundred students in my junior class."

She looked horrified. "I wouldn't like that at all."

"Well, see, that's the thing. I don't know if I'll like being in such a small school."

It was the one part of Mom's plan that I worried about. Would I fit in? Would the students accept someone who talked with a slight drawl and was severely challenged when it came to building a snowman? Would we have anything in common?

Cliques pretty much ran my old high school. With so few students, could they have more than one clique?

More important, could you have a clique of only one person?

3

"*You okay?*" *Nathalie asked.*

"Oh, yeah, I was just . . ." How to explain? "Mom and I talked about the move and I thought I was prepared, but now that I'm here, I'm a little worried about fitting in." I laughed self-consciously. "Bad time to have second thoughts."

It was a radical change in my lifestyle. Cold weather, so few people, no best friend to hook up with at a moment's notice.

"Have you even had a chance to look the town over?" she asked.

"No. I've been on the island less than two hours."

"Come on, then. I'll show you around. That'll make you feel better. I mean, it's not like this is another planet or anything."

We bundled up—or rather *I* bundled up. She just slipped on her coat, not even bothering to button it, and we headed out.

I came from an area of the country with a five-hundred page Mapsco, created to help people find their way through the maze of streets. Here they might have a five-page Mapsco, if that. Our inn is on Main Street, which is pretty much the *main* street. I'd never lived in a place where Main Street was still the main thoroughfare. Back home, Main was in the historic part of downtown, seldom used. It was obvious that here the street name still held significance. It didn't even have traffic lights.

When we got to an intersection, Nathalie pointed. "My street is one over. Come on, I'll show you where I live."

She turned up one block and then down another, which ran parallel to Main.

"Have you always lived here?" I asked.

"Since I was born."

"It's warmer in the summer, right?"

"Lots warmer. You can ride bikes around the island. Skip rocks across the lake." She bumped up against me. "My boyfriend is the stone skipping champ. Thirty-two skips."

"Wow. Is it official? I mean, is there a contest?"

"Oh, yeah. During the lilac festival. This place looks completely different once the lilacs bloom."

She stopped in front of a blue Victorian house. "This is it. I can actually see the back of your house from my bedroom window."

"That's cool. Guess that means I can see yours as well."

"We could learn Morse code and send messages back and forth to each other."

"I'd rather text message."

She laughed. "I guess that would work too." She spun on her heel. "Come on."

We headed back to Main Street. The wind—or I should say the arctic blast—was whistling off the lake.

Whatever happened to global warming?

A horse-drawn sleigh passed by us, heading into what I suppose was considered downtown. I took out my cell phone, took a picture, and immediately sent it to Tara.

"That is so touristy," Nathalie said, her voice chiding.

"Tara's my best friend. I want her to see what I'm seeing. It's kinda like a winter wonderland. So different from what we're used to."

"Still." She shook her head.

"I shouldn't take pictures?"

"Not if you want to fit in."

Well, maybe I just wouldn't take pictures when Nathalie was around, because it was really an amazing place. With so much snow piled up on the sides of the road, I felt like I was walking through a Thomas Kinkade painting.

A few other people were out, some returning from downtown, some heading in that direction. Each person said hi or waved as he or she passed. They were all so friendly.

I suspected that everyone on this island knew everyone. I wondered if a time would ever come when I'd know everyone and everyone would know me. If so, how long would it take?

And would I ever get accustomed to how quiet everything was? Again, no cars, nothing to really make noise, except for the wind passing between houses or slipping through crevices. My nose was too cold to really smell anything, my hands too numb to feel anything.

As we walked along, eventually the houses stopped and buildings designed for commerce began.

I could tell that the street was tourist heaven during the warmer weather, but now many of the stores were closed. One had a sign on the door that read, WILL RETURN AFTER THE FIRST THAW.

I guessed that was a little bit of island humor.

"I know the island is famous for its fudge," I said. "I'd love to get some. Will any of the shops be open?"

"You bet. See Sweet Temptations?" She pointed to a white two-story building. "That's my family's business."

"Oh, cool."

"Not so cool. I have to work with the most annoying guy, because his family is in partnership with mine."

That wasn't good news. I knew there weren't many guys on the island and if one was already identified as a jerk . . . online dating was back on the agenda.

I didn't know what to say except "Bummer."

She made a face, scrunching up her nose. "It's not too bad during the winter, because one person can usually handle things. So we trade days, but during tourist season we both have to work. Usually together."

"What's he do that's so awful?"

"You'll see."

When we got to the shop, I looked in through the window and saw a guy about my age standing in front of a marble table, using a long-handled spatula to turn the fudge over and keep it from sliding off the end. Even from outside, I could smell the aroma of warm fudge.

"Is that him?" I asked.

"Yeah, that's Chase."

Too bad. Because he was really cute. The muscles in his arms were flexing as he moved the spatula.

"Does he have a girlfriend?" I asked.

"Are you kidding? Who would want to date him?"

Maybe me?

Nothing serious, of course. But I did like to have fun, and guys were usually fun.

As we stepped inside, Chase glanced up. "Hey."

He had brown hair and eyes the same shade as the fudge he was stirring. And a killer smile.

"This is Ashleigh," Nathalie said.

"Hey," he said again. "I'm Chase."

"I already told her who you were."

"Well, I didn't know that, now, did I?" He turned his attention back to me. "Want some fudge? All made fresh this morning."

"Yeah, I do," I said, bending down and looking in the case.

"You a fudgie?"

I glanced over my shoulder at him.

"I guess," I answered. "I love fudge."

"No, she's not a fudgie," Nathalie said to him, then to me, "A fudgie is what we call a tourist."

I laughed. "Oh." *I have a lot to learn*, I thought.

Then Nathalie turned back to Chase. "They bought the Shoemakers' place."

"So you're getting into the B&B business," he said to me.

I couldn't figure out what Nathalie found annoying. He seemed like a totally nice guy. And he was hot.

"My mom more than me," I told him. "I'll help where I can, but I'm really not sure how it'll all work. It's so new."

"It'll be an adventure," he said.

"Like you know about adventure. Chase has been working here forever," Nathalie said.

"Not literally forever," Chase said. "First I had to learn how to walk and talk, and then I had to wait until I was tall enough to see over the counter—"

"He's such a smart mouth," Nathalie said, interrupting him. "So what kind of fudge do you want? I'll get it for you."

She walked around behind the counter, and I turned my attention back to the various choices. "What do you recommend?"

"Depends on what you like," Nathalie said.

"We're famous for our marble walnut," Chase said. "White and milk chocolate swirled together with nuts mixed in."

I glanced over at him and smiled. Nathalie's opinion of him baffled me. He wasn't a jerk at all.

"That's what I'll try," I said.

"How much do you want?" Nathalie asked.

"She's new to the island. Give her a pound. My treat," Chase said.

I felt my grin broaden. I never say no to free fudge. Especially when it comes from a hottie.

"Don't be flattered," Nathalie mumbled as she grabbed a tissue and then a hunk of chocolate. "He gives freebies to all the girls. It's the only way he can get a date."

I found that hard to believe. I figured he could have a date anytime he wanted. Of course, there were probably more choices in fudge than in girls on the island.

"Girls are like fudge," Chase said, like he was reading my mind. "You have to sample them all before you settle on your favorite."

He winked at me. I felt an instant connection, because that was the exact same way I felt about dating.

My cheeks grew warm, and I wondered if it would make me look cheap—slutty even—to go out with Chase just to get free fudge. But then, I wanted to go out with him anyway, even without the freebie.

"You are so lame," Nathalie muttered to Chase.

"Nathalie is so predictable," he said to me. "Chocolate pecan. She never tries anything different."

"Don't have to, when you start out with the best," Nathalie said.

Are we really talking about fudge here? I wondered. Because it sure seemed to be a heated conversation if it was about candy.

Maybe because they worked together, they just got on each other's nerves easily.

"I'll pop some divinity in here too," Nathalie said, putting the box of fudge and a small bag of divinity into a larger sack.

"Thanks," I said, taking them from her. "Sure I can't pay you for them?"

"We're sure," Chase said, before Nathalie could answer.

"Thanks again."

"Anytime."

"Not literally anytime," Nathalie said. "We are, after all, a business, and we're supposed to be interested in making a profit."

"She's no fun," Chase said. "I'll bet you're fun."

Were we flirting? Maybe we were flirting.

"I'm a laugh a minute," I said. I laughed. "See? In sixty seconds I'll have another one."

He laughed really loudly, his eyes twinkling.

"You *are* fun."

"Okay, I think we're done here," Nathalie suddenly announced.

"We've been getting orders all morning," Chase said to her. "Why don't you box them for shipping while you're here?"

"Because it's my day off."

"You ship fudge?" I asked.

Nathalie looked back at me. "Sure. You want to ship some somewhere?"

"Yeah, to my friend Tara back home."

"I thought this was home," Chase said.

I shook my head and gave him a wry grin. "Old habits are hard to break."

"I can imagine. I've only ever lived here."

"I think it's going to take more getting used to than I thought."

"You just need someone to show you the ropes, and fortunately for you, I know the ropes really well."

"Shipping the fudge," Nathalie said, in a singsong voice, interrupting our conversation and slapping a form and a pen on the counter. "Fill out the shipping info. I'd do express so it gets there fresh."

I filled out the form, then made my fudge selections. I went with a variety—one quarter pound each of milk chocolate, key lime, rocky road, and chocolate walnut.

"She's going to love these," Nathalie said, closing up the box and taping my order sheet on top of it. "I'll go prepare the shipping label and get this boxed up so it'll go out today."

She disappeared through a doorway.

"Wow, she must really like you," Chase said.

"I like her." I moved back toward the door, back to where he was working, very close to the front window. I guess for tourists he'd be an added attraction.

"Thanks again for the fudge."

"Hey, no problem. Although Nathalie's right, I just give it away to get dates. So when do you want to go out?"

"You're not serious." I'm a firm believer in speed dating, but this was warp speed.

He shrugged. "You got a boyfriend?"

"Well, no."

"Your calendar already filled?"

"I just got here."

"So you're available."

You are available, Ash, I thought.

"You move really fast," I pointed out. I mean, I knew what the guy looked like, but I knew absolutely nothing else about him. Except that Nathalie said he was a jerk. But he didn't seem to be a jerk. Maybe he was one of those psychopathic types who appear normal until the cops take a look in his basement.

"Have to. New chicks don't last long. So can you blame me? The one thing this island lacks is variety in babes."

"How about variety in guys?"

He grinned. "We're lacking in that, too. I could be the best offer you get all winter."

But I had standards, even when it came to dating. I needed a few more details.

"I researched the school. It's going to be so different from what I'm used to. Are you a student there?"

"You bet. Senior. Counting the days until I get off this rock."

"This rock?"

"That's what we call the island when we're not happy with it."

"Why aren't you happy with it?"

He looked toward the door where Nathalie had disappeared. Then he turned his attention back to me. "Let's just say that sometimes it's easy to be invisible."

With so few people, I couldn't imagine it, but I thought maybe more was going on here than I realized.

"So, you wanna go out?" he asked.

"We just met."

"Yeah, but you're a laugh a minute. I like that in a girl."

"I'm not really a laugh a minute."

"That's okay. I don't really give away free fudge for dates." He paused, grinned broadly. "Usually. Come on. Go out with me."

I felt a small thrill. Maybe online dating wasn't going to be in my future after all.

"Where do people go on dates around here?" I asked.

"Lots of places. We could go to V.P."

"V.P.?"

"Village Pub."

"Sounds like a bar."

"Nah, it's where all the kids hang out. Pool, darts, getting together . . . How 'bout Friday night?"

I was in town half a day and I already had a date. How many guys were on this island? And what were the odds that I'd connect with another one as easily as I'd connected with Chase? Amazing.

I gave him a huge smile. "I'm there."

"Great."

I held up my sack. "And to think, I thought I

only came in here for fudge."

"And if you were smart, that's all you'd be leaving with," Nathalie grumbled, coming out from the back room, tugging on mittens.

I just didn't get her objections.

"Friday," I said to Chase, smiling brightly. "Can't wait."

He winked at me. "I'll come by at seven."

Shaking her head, Nathalie grabbed my arm. "Honestly, I don't know what girls see in him. Come on, let's get out of here."

She practically shoved me out the door.

"Bye, Chase. Thanks for the fudge," I called over my shoulder.

When we were outside, Nathalie said, "I have to warn you that Chase is a major player."

She made it sound like I shouldn't have been flattered that he'd asked me out.

"I thought he was nice," I told her.

"I guess. It's just so weird watching him flirt all the time. It really irritates me. And the longest he's ever had a girlfriend is, like, two minutes."

"I didn't think many girls lived on the island," I said.

"He's really into fudgies. No commitment, nothing long-term. Unlike me. I've had the same boyfriend for five years now."

"Awesome." I didn't know anyone who'd had a boyfriend for that long. Gosh, five years? They started dating in middle school? Oh, wait, there was no middle school. There was just school.

"Yeah, we practically grew up together. Of course, I guess that's pretty true of everyone who lives here." She glanced around. "So, do you think you can find your way home from here?"

Her question took me by surprise, but I said, "Sure. No problem."

"Okay, then, I'm going to see my boyfriend. See ya around, girlfriend," she said.

She started walking in the opposite direction that I needed to go. I could see a road curving upward. That might be interesting to explore someday. As a matter of fact, I really needed to map out an exploring strategy. While the island wasn't that large, it still had lots of possibilities.

But I was starting to lose feeling in my extremities again. Maybe in time, I'd toughen up and the cold wouldn't feel so cold.

I glanced around. I could see only a few people, so I took out my cell phone and very nonchalantly sent a few more pictures to Tara. No way did I want to be mistaken for a tourist. This was my new home.

I wanted to do everything I could to fit in.

* * *

"I can't believe there's so much snow!" Tara said when I called her later that night.

"I know. And there's more falling right now."

I was sitting on the window seat in my room, wrapped in a quilt my grandmother had made and wearing my toasty slippers—specially designed to be warmed in the microwave.

"That is so cool. Shaun and I went cycling today—in shorts."

I loved Tara. She'd been my best friend forever. But her selection of boyfriend had baffled me. Shaun Dade. I secretly call him Shaun of the Dead. He never gets excited about *anything*. Well, except maybe dating Tara, but even then it's hard to tell. She told me that he saves his enthusiasm for making out. Way too much information.

"I have a feeling it's going to be a while before I'm wearing shorts again," I said. *If ever!*

"Have you built a snowman yet?"

"Nooo!"

"Why not?"

"Maybe because I'm a little old for building snowmen?"

"You're never too old for building snowmen. Besides, you could build a whole village of snow-men."

Shaking my head, I looked down where the

street lamps were casting a glow. I saw two people walking together, arm in arm, probably trying to warm each other up. This was definitely a place for couples. And I'd already made great progress in that area.

"Guess what? I've got a date already."

"You're kidding!"

She practically shrieked in my ear. She and Shaun were total opposites. Maybe it was true that opposites attract.

"I thought there were, like, no guys on the island," she continued.

"There are guys. Just not many."

"And you've already hooked up with one?"

"Apparently, he has no interest whatsoever in commitment."

"Sounds like a match made in heaven."

"That's the thing. There's no potential for an actual *match*, because neither of us wants a match. That's what makes him perfect. We'll go out a time or two, and he'll move on to the fudgies."

"The what?"

"The tourists."

"What if you don't want him to move on?"

Tara—who thought the ultimate was having a boyfriend—had a difficult time understanding my attitude about dating. It wasn't only because I'd grown up with Mom constantly reminding me to wait. I just didn't seem to have the settle-for-one-guy gene.

"It won't happen," I said with full confidence.

"What if it does?"

"Tara, he likes to go out with different girls. I like to go out with different guys."

"Yeah, but there aren't as many guys on the island as there are here."

"I'll date fudgies, too." As a matter of fact, now that I knew that was an option, I could see the potential for getting to meet all kinds of guys. It could be fun. Lots and lots of fun.

"Okay," she said with a sigh, which I knew meant she wasn't going to try to convince me. So a subject change was coming. "I can't believe your mom named your new place after you."

With my cell phone, I'd taken pictures of the sign and sent them to her. When no one was looking, of course.

"Yeah, I thought that was pretty cool. I'm going to design the website."

I'd taken website design my sophomore year and had been in advanced design before Mom and I decided we wanted to move.

"Awesome," Tara said. "You have something in mind?"

We tossed ideas back and forth until Shaun showed up at her place. Then she hung up to be with him.

I brought my knees up to my chest, wrapped my arms around my legs, and gazed out the window. It really was pretty at night. And so quiet. Except for the wind howling.

I really liked my room, and I was definitely going to keep it.

But just for tonight, I might sleep with the light on.

4

I am so not a morning person. And early morning? Forget it. As far as I'm concerned, it should have never been invented.

I was snuggled in my bed, under a mound of blankets, my head beneath my pillow, trying to ignore the wind shrieking around outside. Because the house was old, it wasn't very well insulated or sealed. Everything seemed to rattle.

I rolled over and sighed. It was still dark and dreary, but my internal clock told me I needed coffee.

Wearing my not-so-sexy flannel trousers and long-sleeved shirt, I clambered out of bed and put on my fuzzy purple slippers. Shivering, I slipped on my thick robe, but didn't bother to tie it. I was going to head quickly down the stairs to the bathroom, where hopefully I could find more warmth, along with my toothbrush and hairbrush.

The stairs did their usual creaking as I hurried

down them. Briefly, I stopped to look through the circular window and saw the silhouette of someone trudging along the street. I wondered how long it would take me to get used to all the snow.

I dashed down the narrow steps. When I got to the bottom of the stairs, I turned into the hallway and came up short.

A lumberjack was standing there.

Or at least, that's what he looked like. A really young, really *hot* lumberjack. He was tall and broad, with midnight black hair that curled around his ears and across his brow, creating the perfect frame for his startling blue eyes.

He was wearing an unbuttoned red plaid flannel shirt that was so thick it was almost a jacket. Beneath that he wore a black turtleneck sweater. He was turned slightly so I couldn't see his other hand.

Lumberjacks carried axes. I had a flashback to *The Shining*. My heart hammered against my ribs. I didn't know this guy. Who was he? And where was Mom?

He grinned. "Hey."

"Who are you?" I snapped, jerking the sides of my robe together and tying the sash.

His eyebrows shot up. "Most people I know respond to a greeting with another greeting."

"Well, I'm not someone you know, now, am I? For all I know you're a serial killer."

He chuckled. How could anyone chuckle in the morning?

"Do I look like a serial killer?" he asked.

I guessed not, but still . . .

"What are you doing here?" I demanded.

"Your mom hired my dad to do some repairs. They're in the kitchen discussing details."

"So you just decided to make yourself at home?"

He narrowed his eyes. "Your mom said I could look around. I've never been in this house before, but it's always interested me because of the turrets. I have this thing for turrets. I'm Josh Wynter, by the way."

"And do you become Josh Summer in June?" I asked.

Okay, it was totally lame, a stupid thing to say, but I was still reeling from the fact that a hot guy— were all the guys on this island hot?—was roaming the halls and I was . . .

Not at my best. Ratty robe. Fuzzy slippers. Hair tangled. Teeth unbrushed.

And have I mentioned that I am not a morning person?

"Actually," he said at last, as though finally catching on to my not-so-witty banter, "I stay Josh

Wynter all year. Do you stay unfriendly?"

"That does not deserve an answer," I mumbled as I shoved past him as quickly as I could and went into the bathroom. I slammed the door shut.

Okay, I *had* been unfriendly, rude even, but he was so unexpected. And so hot. And I already had a date for Friday night.

What was I supposed to do? Flirt with him? Would that make me the island slut? Nathalie had been dating the same guy for years! Was that how it worked here?

I stayed with my ear pressed to the door until I heard him walk off, down the stairs. At least, it sounded like he was going down to the second floor, but everything echoed around here. What if he was, in fact, on his way *up* to my room?

I wish I'd told him that his "looking around" ended on the third floor. Although based on my behavior, he probably figured that out.

I pressed my back to the door and slid to the floor.

I had overreacted. Totally. He'd scared me. But not in the ax murderer kind of way.

I'd never before felt such an . . . *attraction* to a guy. Sure, Chase was hot and he was fun and I was looking forward to our date. But I wasn't worried about what he thought of me. When I met him, my heart hadn't pounded so hard that I thought I'd crack a rib. I hadn't been nervous.

That's what I'd been in the hallway just then. Nervous. I'd never been so unsettled around a guy. So why this one?

It didn't make sense. I'd always been cool around guys.

It didn't help matters that when I finally got to my feet and looked in the mirror, I was reminded of my unflattering appearance. I'd given Josh Wynter the worst impression of me in every way imaginable.

Why did I feel such overwhelming disappointment?

When I got back to my bedroom, I looked out the window. No truck out in the street. I'd almost decided that meant that our visitors were gone . . . before I remembered that they wouldn't have a truck. So how would they haul their carpentry materials?

But more important, how would I know when they'd left? I wouldn't hear a vehicle revving up its engine before being driven away. How would I ever hear people arrive or leave?

Obviously the doorbell chime couldn't be heard up here.

Sometime later, I dressed in my jeans and a

bulky cable-knit sweater. I was still wearing my fuzzy slippers as I made my way cautiously downstairs, checking for the Wynter guy, really hoping that I wasn't going to run into him.

I made it safely to the first floor without running into anyone. I glanced into the library and the parlor—all clear.

I needed my coffee—badly. So I had to risk a visit to the kitchen, where I might indeed find people.

But I didn't. I found only Mom, and while she's technically a person, she's one I know.

She was standing in front of the window, gazing out at the wintery backyard, one of her precious china cups in her hand. She glanced over her shoulder. "Coffee's ready."

"Great!"

I grabbed my favorite mug. It was blue and huge, twice the size of a normal mug, and said on the side, "Still not enough." Tara had given it to me.

I filled it to the brim, added a little milk, stirred in some sugar, and practically inhaled my first sip, relishing the flavor. Then I moved to the window, pressed my hip against the counter, and looked outside.

"Uh, Mom, do you think in the future, you

could let me know when we're going to have company in the morning?" I asked.

She finally looked at me then. Really looked at me. "Was there a problem?"

"Only running into someone I didn't know before I was ready to be presented to the world."

She smiled wryly. "Sorry. Mr. Wynter finished up a project earlier than expected, so he had time this morning to drop by to discuss some of the remodeling I want done. They're going to start tomorrow."

"They?" My stomach knotted up.

"He and his son." She looked back out the window. "I can't believe how pristine the snow is."

She wanted to talk snow and I wanted to talk . . .

"So what do you know about his son?"

Mom shook her head. "Not a lot. His name is Josh. He goes to school here."

Great. That was so not what I wanted to hear.

"Do you know what grade he's in?"

"No, we didn't really discuss personal things." She studied me. "Are you sure everything is all right?"

"Yeah. Sure."

"He seemed nice."

"He was. I wasn't."

"That doesn't sound like you."

"I wasn't awake yet."

It was a lame excuse. I knew it. Mom knew it.

"I'm sure you'll get a chance to apologize," she said, moving away from the counter.

That's what worried me. Seeing him again, trying to figure out what to say. I *never* had a problem figuring out what to say to guys. This was so weird, so unlike me. Maybe it was the cold. Maybe it had killed off some brain cells.

"I noticed it snowing last night. I guess I need to shovel the snow off the walk."

Mom gave me another wry grin. "No. Josh already did it. See? Nice guy."

Totally nice guy. Maybe too nice.

My instincts were sending out some sort of warning.

Too bad it was sending it out in a secret code that I couldn't decipher.

Shortly after lunch our stuff arrived on a wagon with runners. A burly guy who didn't even bother wearing a jacket carted all the boxes into the house.

In my bedroom two hours later, I had half a dozen boxes opened, trying to figure out where to put things so they looked *right*. But nothing really looked right here yet.

I didn't want to duplicate my room back in Texas, but I wanted to feel like this room was truly mine. It was just so different from what I'd had before, though. As much as I loved it, I wanted some of my former life to fit. As much as I'd wanted this adventure, I hadn't expected to miss the familiar so much.

And it didn't make the unpacking go any quicker because I kept staring off into space and thinking about Josh Wynter. Maybe I could convince him that he'd met my evil twin or something.

"Hiya!"

I jerked back to the present. I was on the bed arranging various stuffed animals I'd collected over the years. Nathalie stood in the doorway, two girls beside her.

"Your mom said we could come on up," she said.

"Oh, great. I was just"—I slid off the bed—"trying to figure out where to put things."

"These are my best friends." Nathalie left it at that, like maybe they were nameless, or she couldn't remember their names.

"I'm Shanna," one girl said. Her hair—the color of the charcoal briquettes my dad used in his grill back home—hung thick and straight past her shoulders. "And this is Corey."

I couldn't tell much about Corey. Her hair was all stuffed beneath her knitted red cap, but based on her fair features I thought she was probably blond. Then again, maybe she had dark hair and was only sun-deprived. I wasn't familiar enough with this world yet to make assumptions.

"I told them all about you," Nathalie said.

"Like what, exactly?"

"Oh, you know, like you're from Texas, but you don't have a drawl. You're my new best friend—"

I was? That was a nice thing to say.

"—and that you have the most totally awesome bedroom. And of course, they wanted to see it, so here we are!"

"Yeah," Shanna said. "Nathalie said maybe we could have a sleepover sometime."

"That'd be great." And I realized I actually thought it would be.

"Oh, and I told them that you don't have a boyfriend."

"The island is not the place to be if you don't have a boyfriend," Corey said.

"Do you have boyfriends?" I asked.

"Oh, yeah," Corey said.

I didn't want to have to explain my stance on not getting serious yet, so I just said, "Well, I am going out with a guy—"

"Yeah, I heard," Corey said. "My brother."

"Chase is your brother?"

"Yeah." She walked to the rounded window and looked out. "I can see only a small portion of the lake from my room because of the row of houses in front of us. I have to turn my head at an awkward angle and cross my eyes to see between the houses."

"Sorry 'bout that," I said, figuring I was living in the row of houses in front of her.

"She's just messing with you," Shanna said.

"So she can see the lake?" I asked.

"No, but she doesn't care about a view. I mean, it's not like you have to walk far to see the lake. We're in the middle of it, after all."

"We were thinking of going to the mall," Nathalie said. "Did you want to come with us?"

"There's a mall here?" I asked.

Hallelujah!

My dad was always saying that Tara and I should get frequent shopper points for all the time we spent at the mall. The Galleria in Dallas was my favorite, by far, but I never turned away a chance to go to a mall. Any mall.

"Of course we have a mall," Nathalie said. "We have four, actually."

"How do we get there?" I asked.

"We walk."

The mall we went to was in the shopping district. It was small, with no department stores, but it did have several interesting shops. More like boutiques. Very specialized.

Shopping with Nathalie and her friends—who were quickly becoming my friends—was a lot like shopping with Tara. We tried on more clothes than we'd ever buy. As a matter of fact, I ended up being the only one who bought anything—some fur-lined, knee-high boots and a couple of thick woolen sweaters.

After we'd shopped until we were almost ready to drop, we stopped in a little bakery. We each bought a slice of cake and some hot chocolate. Then we sat at a round table near the window.

"This is so good," I said, sipping the hot chocolate. "I have a feeling I'm only going to be drinking warm beverages from now on."

"You'll get used to the cold," Shanna said.

"And the weather is really nice in the summer," Corey said. "The island is perfect for nature lovers."

"Well, summer can't get here fast enough, as

far as I'm concerned," I said. "I mean, I knew it would be cold—"

"This isn't really all that cold," Corey said.

"It's freezing!" I said. "With the wind chill, it's twenty degrees."

Corey shrugged. "Well, yeah, but it can get colder."

I shivered.

"Like I said, you'll get used to it," Shanna assured me. "We barely notice the cold. So what do you do for fun if there's no snow around?"

"Shop, go to concerts, see movies. You know. Stuff."

Shanna leaned forward. "So tell us about the guys in Texas. They're hot, right?"

"Oh, yeah. Especially in the summer when the temperature is, like, a hundred degrees."

"That's not what I meant!" Shanna said.

I grinned, then told them about the guys I knew back home.

5

The next morning, I threw on baggy sweats before leaving my bedroom. Fortunately, I didn't run into any surprises on my way to the bathroom. After brushing my teeth, combing my hair, and making myself feel halfway decent—I needed coffee to feel completely decent—I headed downstairs.

And there was Josh Wynter, on the second floor, lugging a rolled tarp into one of the bedrooms. He stopped in the doorway, studying me.

I shifted from one slippered foot to the other. "Good morning," I grumbled.

He glanced around, pointed a thumb at his chest. "You talking to me?"

I rolled my eyes. "I'm not a morning person, okay?"

"No offense, but in that case, living in a bed-and-breakfast is probably not the way to go."

"I know. I'm trying to talk my mom into

changing it into a bed-and-dinner."

He laughed. He had a great laugh. A deep rumble that made my toes curl inside my fuzzy socks. Weird. Guys never made my toes curl.

I angled my head thoughtfully. "I could probably even do a bed-and-lunch."

Laughing more, he leaned against the doorjamb. His blue eyes were sparkling now. His eyes seemed even bluer because of his dark hair.

"I don't even eat breakfast," I confessed.

"It's the most important meal of the day."

"So what are you, a nutritionist?"

"Nah. A TV watcher. It's amazing the useless bits of information you can pick up watching TV."

"Well, if they said it on TV, it's gotta be true."

His grin broadened. Did the guy ever stop smiling once he got started? And what did it say about my morning persona that I was irritated by his smile—and by the fact that he was incredibly good-looking? In a horror movie, he'd definitely be the one who survived.

He almost made me regret having a date Friday night. Every girl I'd met so far had a boyfriend. Would I be the only girl interested in dating different guys? Would that stop me from fitting in? And would one or two dates with Josh be enough? Would it satisfy my craving to be with him?

Wait, craving? I never felt that way about anyone. It was like someone I didn't know had taken possession of my thoughts.

"I've gotta get some coffee," I mumbled.

"Don't let me stop you."

"I won't."

I shuffled by him. Peering into the room, I could see that all the furniture had been moved into its center. How long had he been here? Obviously quite a while. He'd probably had coffee *and* breakfast already.

"Don't let me stop *you* from working," I said.

"I won't," he said.

He walked into the room, and I hurried down the stairs. At the bottom, I was surprised to hear laughter weaving into the entryway. My mom's laughter. Light and airy.

It was really too early in the morning for light and airy, but I was rooted to the spot. I couldn't remember the last time I'd heard Mom laugh with such abandon. Then she giggled. "Oh, Ralph."

Ralph? Who the heck was Ralph?

I strode through the dining room and into the kitchen. Mom was sitting at the table beside a man I assumed was Mr. Wynter, because he looked a lot like Josh. Wearing guilty expressions, they both looked up when I walked in.

"Hey, hon," Mom said. "Help yourself to coffee, then you can pick out some wallpaper for your bedroom."

I grabbed my usual morning mug and poured coffee, milk, and sugar into it. Leaning against the counter, I took a sip and began to feel more human. "I heard you laughing. What was so funny?"

"Mr. Wynter was just telling me a story about one of his customers."

"Isn't there, like, some sort of customer/carpenter privilege?"

I didn't want to think about the nasty things that Josh could tell people about me.

Mr. Wynter actually turned bright red. "Uh, well, uh . . . it wasn't anything . . . it wasn't a secret."

"Don't worry about it, Dad," Josh said, suddenly appearing in the doorway. "She's just worried that we'll tell people she's not a morning person."

How had he figured that out?

"We'll sign a nondisclosure statement," he added. "Although truthfully, it's pretty obvious."

"Thanks . . . I think," I said, before taking a big gulp of coffee.

"Ashleigh, pour Josh some coffee," Mom said.

"That's okay," Josh said, walking around me and grabbing a mug from the mug tree. "I'm not a guest."

He winked at me. My toes did that whole crazy curling thing again and my heart started fluttering like a bird trapped in my chest. *What is up with that?* I thought. I'm always cool, calm, and collected around guys, but then, I never felt like anything was at stake before. Why did I feel like something was at stake here? My attitude about guys had always been like 'em and leave 'em—at least until I'm out of college. But I had a feeling that Josh Wynter would be a hard guy to leave.

Josh leaned one hip against the counter and sipped his black coffee.

"Ashleigh, come look at the wallpaper selections," Mom said.

Good. A distraction. That was what I needed. I sat at the table and started looking through the binder.

"Have lots of this in stock," Mr. Wynter said, pointing to a swatch of wallpaper.

Josh cleared his throat. I glanced over at him. He slowly shook his head. It looked like he was fighting back another grin.

Maybe because the wallpaper his dad wanted me to select was a puke green with mallard ducks on it. Not that I had anything against ducks, but puke green? I could certainly understand why he had a lot in stock. Who would want it? What I couldn't understand was the reason he'd ordered it in the first place.

"That's not really me," I said carefully.

"How 'bout this? We have this striped stuff. . . ."

That looked like drunk candy canes. Hard to explain, but trust me.

"Uh, no—"

"Dad, why don't you just let her look?"

His dad looked disgruntled, but then the wrinkles on his face eased. "I guess there's no hurry. We have plenty to keep us busy with the guestrooms."

"Speaking of the guestrooms," Mom said, "I'd like to run an idea I had for one of them by you. Would you mind coming upstairs?"

"Not at all," Mr. Wynter said. He shoved himself out of his chair and followed Mom out of the kitchen.

She'd mentioned putting a window seat with a storage area in one of the rooms that had a view of the lake. I had a feeling she was going to keep the Wynters busy all winter. I smiled at that thought and went back to looking at the samples of wallpaper.

"If you don't see anything you like, you can go

to the hardware store down the street," Josh said. "They have a bigger selection, not in stock, but that can be ordered. We can get it from the mainland."

I looked over at him. "Won't it be more expensive?"

"Yeah. Dad tends to buy stuff on closeout. It never occurs to him there's a reason stuff is on closeout—like, no one wanted it to begin with."

"You mean, you don't think ducks sitting in puke was someone's first choice?"

"Probably not."

He grinned. Really broadly. He had a nice smile, a very friendly smile. Not teasing, not flirtatious like Chase's. It was just . . . nice. And I thought I could look at it forever and never grow tired of it.

Whoa! Slow down, Ash.

I needed to get out of there.

I closed the book. "I don't know that I really need or want wallpaper. I'd love to have some shelves, though."

"Those are easy enough to make. Shoot, I could make those tonight. No problem."

"I don't know. My room is very oddly shaped."

"I just have to take some measurements."

"It's the room at the top of the stairs, right off the third floor."

"I sorta figured that out yesterday."

From where I was sitting, it looked like he was blushing, but maybe it was just the way the sun was coming through the window that he was now looking out of. Was he embarrassed thinking about our encounter? I'd been the one still in PJ's.

"How long do you think all this work is going to take?" I asked.

Josh looked at me and shrugged. "You in a hurry?"

I shrugged back. "Having company this early messes up my morning routine."

"What's your routine?"

"The usual girl routine."

"It's just me and Dad. I'm not real familiar with the usual girl routine."

"What about your mom?"

"She got tired of the winters."

I couldn't help myself. I gave him a mischievous grin. "You mean, the winters like the cold and snow, or the Wynters, like father and son?"

"Both, I guess."

I didn't know what to say. I'd been teasing, but apparently . . .

He set his mug on the counter. "I need to get back to painting that room."

He started to walk out. I got up so fast that I

nearly toppled the chair and lost my balance.

"I was just teasing. I didn't mean anything. I didn't think she'd really *left* left."

He furrowed his brow. "So what did you think?"

"That she didn't like the cold, maybe went to Florida for the winter or something. You know. Short-term getaway."

"Nope. Long-term getaway. Been about ten years now."

"I'm sorry."

"No big deal. Hell, I don't even remember what she looks like."

Before I had a chance to remove one foot from my mouth and jam the other one in, he walked out of the kitchen.

6

Why was I always saying idiotic things around Josh? I'd always been as comfortable around boys as I was around girls. Best buds and all that. But then, I'd always known best buds was all we'd ever be. Nothing serious. Why did thoughts of being serious keep popping into my mind?

Why did I care so much what Josh thought of me? My whole reaction to him was totally strange.

Part of me wanted to avoid him, but he was going to be in my house constantly until the work was completed. I didn't want to be creeping around, dreading running into him. I was going to have to face him.

I took my coffee mug to the sink and rinsed it out. While I was standing there, Mom and Mr. Wynter came back into the kitchen. Mom was laughing again, lightly. Clearly she'd found something he said amusing. I wondered if he was flirting, if maybe I should tell Mom that his wife had left him.

Not that Mr. Wynter looked like a player. He was big and burly, with thick black hair like his son's and a short beard that made him look like a large, cuddly teddy bear. He wore overalls over a plaid flannel shirt. Not really player material.

"Did you make a decision?" Mom asked now. "About the wallpaper?"

"Not really. Can I think about it for a while?"

"Sure," Mr. Wynter said. "We're seldom in a hurry around here. That's the beauty of island life."

"Thanks."

"I thought we might practice serving tea this afternoon. I found a recipe for watercress and cheddar sandwiches," Mom said. "Don't those sound lovely?"

"Uh, I guess." I was a burger girl.

"What do you think, Mr. Wynter?" Mom asked.

"Sounds great to me."

He grinned at her. I had a feeling she could have suggested dirt mixed with autumn leaves and he'd have said it sounded great.

"I've still got a few boxes to unpack so I'm gonna go . . ." I fluttered my hand and then made a hasty retreat.

Once I started up the stairs, I was hit with the smell of fresh paint. My instincts screamed for me to simply walk on past that first bedroom, get to my room as soundlessly and quietly as possible. And that's what I'd planned to do. But as I went past, I peered inside.

Josh was using a long-handled roller to apply a creamy yellow to the wall. Like mine, this room wasn't wallpapered.

He'd covered the furniture with the tarp I'd seen him lugging inside. He turned to dip the roller into the paint pan and froze as he caught sight of me.

"My dad left us," I felt compelled to say.

He seemed to think about that. Then finally he asked, "How could he have left you when he was never here?"

"Well, first he left, and then we left." I shook my head, as if doing so would clear it. "He left my mom about two years ago. We left because he's about to get remarried."

"Bummer."

"Totally."

He gave me a small grin. I smiled back.

"I'm not sure what's worse," I confessed. "You not remembering your mom or me not being able to forget my dad. I really miss him."

That was something I could never tell my mom, because it would just make her feel guilty. And telling it to a guy I'd just met—a guy I didn't know well—was weird for me. While I'd dated several guys, I wasn't in the habit of baring my soul to them or sharing secrets.

"Anyway, I just . . ." I did the whole flapping my hand thing again, like I thought that was the way to create words. I gave up and just shrugged. "Thought I should say something, because I'm sure your mom liked you and it was the cold, not—"

"Hey, forget it. Like I said, I don't even remember her."

I couldn't imagine that. "Not at all?"

"Want to help me paint?" he asked.

I didn't blame him for the abrupt subject change. It was more polite than telling me to butt out of his business.

I narrowed my eyes. "Isn't my mom paying *you* to paint?"

"Actually, she's paying my dad."

"Who no doubt pays you."

He grinned. "Sometimes. What else have you got to do?"

"You tell me. This is your island. Seriously, what is there to do around here?"

"Lots." He finally got around to dipping the

roller into the pan and started painting the wall again.

"Care to share?"

"Cross-country skiing is wildly popular."

"Slight problem there. I've never been on skis."

"You're kidding."

"Hello? Texas? We don't get a lot of snow."

"I can't imagine." He glanced over at me. "What's winter without snow?"

"Warm."

He laughed really deeply, shaking his head. "I don't see the point."

"Well, I'm having a bit of a problem seeing the point to winter."

He arched a brow.

"The season," I added. I was beginning to see a point to Josh *Wynter*. He was someone to talk to.

"Is your dad a comedian or something?" I asked.

He turned around, grinning. What was it with the Wynter guys that they were always grinning?

"Actually, he does a stand-up routine down at one of the pubs on amateur night." He grimaced. "It's pretty bad. Why?"

I shrugged. "My mom seems to laugh a lot when he's around. I guess he's practicing."

"Not if she's laughing. Trust me. No one laughs

at his jokes. They're pretty lame. But for some reason, he knows how to make our customers laugh."

"So my mom's not special?" Was Mr. Wynter going to break her heart?

"He likes people to be happy. Why get bent out of shape about that?"

"I'm not bent." I resented that he thought I was. "I'm just not used to hearing my mom laugh so much."

"You say that like laughter's a bad thing."

It was if my mom got hurt. I sighed. She was a big girl, she could take care of herself. After all, she'd survived a major breakup.

"You should try it sometime," he added.

"I'll have you know I laugh plenty."

"I don't think *plenty* means what you think it does. It means often, a lot—"

"I know what it means. I'm a laugh a minute. Ha, ha. And I'll laugh again in another minute."

He just stared at me like I'd totally lost my mind. Maybe I had. Chase had thought I was cute when I'd said almost the same thing. I didn't know why it had worked with him and not Josh. Time for a serious subject change.

"So, are you, like, one of the five students in the junior class?"

I'd researched the single school on the island so I knew that each classroom had two grade levels in it—until eighth grade. So students at different levels intermingled a lot more here than they did back home.

"Nope. I'm one of the six in the senior class."

Oh, an older guy. Intriguing. I crossed my arms, leaned against the wall.

He grimaced. "You probably shouldn't have done that."

"Oh, shoot!" I pulled away from the wall, bringing a good deal of the paint with me. "You could have posted a sign."

"I thought it was pretty obvious that wet paint was going on the walls."

"Well, still . . ."

He placed his hand on my shoulder. "Step aside."

I did as he ordered, watching while he rolled fresh paint over the mess I'd made.

"I'm going to go change," I mumbled.

"Let me know when you're ready and I'll come to your room."

My heart thudded. "Excuse me?"

"To take measurements for those shelves."

"You were serious about making them?" I asked.

"Sure."

"Okay, then."

"Don't get too excited."

"What do you want me to do? Hug you?"

His eyes seemed to darken, then he shook his head and turned back to the pan. "Just holler when it's okay for me to come up."

I backed up a step. "Give me ten."

"Ten?"

"Minutes. Just come up in ten minutes."

Which, under normal circumstances, was all I would have needed, except my cell phone was ringing when I got to my room. I took off my paint-splattered clothes as fast as I could and answered the phone right before it went to voice-mail. It was Tara.

"Hey," I said, holding the phone to my ear with one hand, while scrounging through a stack of clothes on a chair with the other.

"The fudge arrived and omigod!" she exclaimed. I could hear her eating. "It's amazing."

I laughed. "I figured you'd like it. The street is lined with fudge shops, but since Nathalie works in one, I'm not sure how I can try out the others without being disloyal."

"Wear a disguise, because you are *obligated* to try every one. It's, like, the law or something."

"Or something. You just want more fudge."

"You bet. So how are things up there?" she asked.

"Cold."

"Are you going to say that every time we talk?" she asked.

"Well, it's *really* cold right now, because I'm half naked." I yanked a pair of sweats free from the pile and managed to pull them on, while holding the phone between my head and shoulder.

"Are you just now getting up?"

Unlike me, Tara's a morning person. She loves dawn. Go figure.

"No, I ran into some wet paint."

"Huh?"

I explained about Mom's renovations, how I came to have paint on my clothes, and that Josh was coming up so I really needed to cover up the old birthday suit.

"So is he hot?" Tara asked.

"It's too cold for anyone up here to be hot," I said, digging out a shirt.

She groaned.

"Hold on." I set down the phone and pulled on my shirt, just as a knock sounded. I picked up the phone, opened the door, waved Josh in, and went back to talking. "I'm back."

"Is he there now?"

"Yes."

I'd never had a guy in my bedroom. My heart started thundering again, but it had to be the situation, not the actual guy.

"So why are you still on the phone?" Tara asked.

"Because—"

"Shouldn't you be trying to hook up with him?"

Him was walking around my room, looking at my various candles. I had one that sounded like a crackling fire when it burned. It was my favorite. I also had lots of little fuzzy toy mice and china figurines of cute rodents.

Josh was looking at things like he thought the assortment was odd. Maybe he'd never been in a girl's room before.

"I mean, that's your usual modus operandi—date, date, date."

Tara still didn't get my whole no-boyfriend-until-I'm-older attitude. Which was fine. I still didn't get her whole hooking-up-with-Shaun-of-the-Dead thing, so that made us even.

"Yeah, I need to go." Even if I wasn't exactly sure if I should be flirting with Josh.

I snapped my phone closed. "My friend Tara."

"Can't be a very close friend if she doesn't

know you well enough not to call before noon."

"Ha-ha, very funny."

He grinned, still glancing around. "You like mice?"

"You say that like it's weird."

"I just picture most girls screaming and squealing whenever they see a mouse."

"I'm not most girls."

"I guess not." He seemed to think about that for a while, or maybe he was thinking about the room, because he suddenly said, "I see what you mean about the shape. This is kinda wasted space." He went to the rear of the room, where the roof slanted down. From his shirt pocket, he pulled out a small notebook and pen. He held them toward me. "You write down the measurements."

Using a rolled metal measuring tape, he began calling out numbers. When he was done, the tape snapped back into the roll with a loud *thwap*.

He duckwalked out until he could stand up straight. He was quite a bit taller than me. I had to look up at him when he took the notepad back. He wrote some things down on it.

"What color?" he asked.

"What?"

He looked up. "What color do you want the shelves?"

"Uh . . ," I shrugged. "White? Brown? I really don't care. You don't even have to paint them—"

"Wynter Warranty. Everything done to your satisfaction."

"How much are these going to cost?"

"Don't worry about it. And don't worry about the color, either. I'll take care of it."

"I wasn't *worried* exactly."

We stood there, looking at each other like there should be something else to say. Having a guy in my bedroom made it seem so much smaller.

He jerked his thumb over his shoulder. "Guess I'd better get back to painting. Sure you don't want to help?"

"Actually," I said, surprising myself with the words that followed, "I do."

"Know anything about stenciling?" he asked when we got back to the guestroom.

I remembered that Mom had mentioned putting borders along the walls near the ceilings in some rooms. "I know what it is, but I've never done it."

"I'll bet you're a natural."

He shoved a ladder over to the portion of the wall that was already painted. He found a stencil— one that Mom had picked out, I guessed—and climbed the ladder. Reaching into a huge pocket on the leg of his coveralls, he brought out a roll of masking tape and secured the stencil in place. He hopped to the floor.

"Climb on up," he ordered, before moving to another part of the room where cans of paint were lined up like good little soldiers.

"What if I mess it up?" I asked.

"Won't happen," he said. He was crouched, pouring purple paint onto a small plate.

"For all you know, I have no talent at painting."

He glanced over at me. "If you screw up, I'll paint over it. It's no big deal."

Not exactly what I'd wanted him to say. Actually, I guess I was looking for some sort of praise, something like—

"Besides, I wouldn't have offered to let you do it if I didn't think you *could* do it," he added.

Okay. That was more along the lines of what I wanted to hear.

Why do you care if he's impressed, Ash? You've got a date with another guy. And they're bound to be friends.

Before moving to the island, it had been easy to have dates with different guys, because there were so many of them—and the odds were good they wouldn't be friends. Chase and Josh had to be friends. Dating both of them wouldn't work.

So Josh Wynter wasn't even on the menu to sample. I'd already chosen the entrée: Chase.

Still, I kicked off my fuzzies and climbed up the ladder.

The ceiling was high, like maybe a thousand feet. Okay, closer to ten, but still . . . The ladder was a little shaky, especially when Josh started to climb it.

"Uh . . . what are you doing?" I asked.

"Coming up to show you how to do it."

And suddenly he was there, his arms coming around me as he put the plate of paint and a brush on the top step of the ladder. Or was it the top of the ladder? Would I really want to stand on the very top of the ladder with nothing to hold on to?

I was obsessing about the ladder and what its various parts were called because that was a lot safer than thinking about the fact that Josh and I were so close. He smelled really good. Not like paint, as I'd expected.

He smelled like a lumberjack, like pine. Woodsy. And even though it was winter, his skin had a brown hue, so I figured in the summer, he spent a lot of time outdoors. He looked the type.

"Are you listening?" he asked.

"Huh?" I sounded breathless. Probably because I was. Having his chest pressed to my back felt so good. I grew warm, kinda dizzy. Maybe it was the height. But I didn't think so.

"I've been showing you how to prepare the brush, how to make sure you don't have too much paint," he said.

I nodded. "I got it."

"You can either dab or swirl," he said, leaning forward to show me.

Which put him even closer, close enough that it was almost an embrace. So close that my mouth went dry.

"Personally"—he cleared his throat—"I like the swirl."

He was giving me other pointers, but I was barely listening. All I could think about was the swirl. The type of swirl that might take place if we were kissing.

7

Only, we weren't kissing. I was amazed by how much I wished we were. I wondered if he had a girlfriend. He hadn't mentioned one. But would he get this close to another girl if he did?

On the other hand, I hadn't mentioned my date with Chase. But a date . . . well, dates came and went in my life.

"Want to give it a try?" he asked.

He held the brush in front of my face. I made a fist to stop my hand from shaking before I took it from him.

"It's okay to paint over the stencil," he said.

I nodded quickly. "I think I've got it."

"Are you afraid of heights?"

"No, why?"

"Because you're shaking."

"I'm just a little cold. Not used to the weather yet."

Cold? What a lie! I was practically burning up.

"Then I definitely don't want you on my snow volleyball team."

"Snow volleyball?"

"Yeah, me and the guys are gonna play later this afternoon. You could come watch us."

Was he asking me out? Should I tell him about Chase?

"You know," he added, "meet people. Besides, studies have shown that staying indoors can lead to depression."

"And emergency rooms have shown that staying outdoors can lead to frostbite, loss of limbs, and freezing to death."

"Only if you're careless."

I shook my head. "It's so cold out there."

"Not once you get used to it."

"You know, if you ever went to Texas you'd probably complain about the heat."

"I never complain about weather. It is what it is."

"You'd complain." I twisted around slightly to make a point—and I'm absolutely certain it was a very valid point and would have nailed his butt—but he was so close and his blue eyes were sparkling as if he were amused . . .

And then they weren't.

They got totally serious. And he dipped his

gaze to my lips. That started them tingling. My body got hotter. How would I explain being taken to the ER with a case of heat stroke?

I wanted to laugh, but this wasn't funny. It was, like, maybe we both realized that being up there on the ladder together, so close together, wasn't a smart move.

Because we had nowhere to go except toward each other and then figuring out if we preferred the dab or the swirl.

And we'd barely had a conversation, but here I was, certain he was going to kiss me.

I watched as his Adam's apple slid up and down.

"Um, so, think you're okay with the stenciling?" he asked.

His voice sounded like he hadn't had anything to drink in years. Dry and scratchy.

I nodded. "I think so."

To my utter mortification, I didn't sound much better.

"Okay, then, I'll leave you to it."

Only, he stayed where he was, looking at me like he'd never really seen me before. Like maybe he was under a spell. I didn't want him to go, but I didn't want him to stay. For the first time in my life, when it came to a guy, I was confused about what I wanted.

"Are *you* afraid of heights?" I asked, to jar us out of whatever was happening here.

"What?"

"You're not leaving."

"Right." He shook his head, grinned. "Right."

Then he climbed down the ladder.

I took a deep breath, not realizing until that moment that I hadn't been breathing.

It got really quiet as I worked on the stenciling. He went back to painting the wall. It was kinda weird because I kept thinking that this would always be *our* room, even when strangers stayed in it. It was the room where we'd talked and worked together. The room where a spark between us almost got started.

But since the spark hadn't ignited, we shared an awkward silence.

"So, this snow volleyball . . . What do you do? Toss snowballs at each other and swat them back and forth?" I asked.

He laughed a little too loudly, like maybe he was as uncomfortable with whatever had almost happened on the ladder as I was.

"No. It's just volleyball. You know volleyball, right?"

"Yeah, I know volleyball. But it's never included the element of snow, so I'm just trying to picture how it works."

"You know anything about beach volleyball?"

I glanced over my shoulder. He was watching me instead of painting. I felt a small thrill at the realization that I had his attention.

"Yes, I know beach volleyball."

"So imagine snow instead of sand."

I went further than that. I imagined everyone bundled up, rolling around trying to get the ball. Athletic ability was certain to be lacking. I snickered at the thought. "I don't see how it can be very competitive."

"It's entertaining, if nothing else. Come and watch us play," he said. "We'll be on the beach—"

"There is no beach," I reminded him.

"There is in the summer. We use the beach volleyball nets. You'll be able to see us from your window, but it's better up close."

It had definitely been better with him up close on the ladder.

He suddenly seemed nervous, maybe thinking the same thing I was, and started rolling the paint over the wall very quickly, almost obsessively, like *get this done and get out of here.*

"I think Mom's planning on us practicing to

have a tea party this afternoon," I said.

"Oh, that'll be *way* more fun," he said, his voice dripping with sarcasm.

I laughed, because he was so right. And what girl in her right mind would willingly choose watercress and cheddar sandwiches over watching hot guys play volleyball, even if they'd look like the Michelin tire guy while doing it?

He turned to look at me. "I like your laugh."

Which made me stop laughing, because something in his eyes told me he liked more than just my laughter.

As though neither of us knew quite what to do with this attraction, we both returned to painting—furiously.

We'd be finished before teatime.

Thinking about watching Josh play volleyball gave me very little patience for sitting down for tea. Afternoon tea is supposed to be calm and relaxing, but all I wanted was for it to be over with.

I stood in the kitchen, cutting crusts off the bread of our cream cheese, cheddar cheese, and watercress sandwiches.

"I want to find a summertime drink to offer in the afternoons," Mom said.

"How 'bout lemonade?"

"That's so unoriginal. I was thinking something more unique." Mom took a bite of the sandwich, which she'd cut into little triangles.

Any other time, I probably would have thought the tiny sandwiches were cute. But I had watching-a-cute-guy on the brain. And cute guy always wins out over cute sandwiches.

"It's pretty good," Mom said.

I took a bite. It was.

Mom took a Post-it note and drew three stars on it. She had a cookbook system: three stars—like it, want to serve it again; two stars—it's okay in a pinch; one star—tried it once, never again. She slapped the Post-it on the page in her *Teatime* cookbook. "One down, about two hundred to go."

I was horrified. "We're not going to make all those sandwiches, are we?"

"Well, no, not all of them, but we need to have a nice selection, and I certainly don't want to serve something I haven't tasted. And then there are all the yummy desserts."

Speaking of yummy . . .

Now was probably the time to tell Mom that I wanted to cut the teatime short.

The doorbell rang.

"I'll get it," I said, hopping out of the chair.

"Wonder who it could be," Mom murmured.

It was Nathalie.

"Heard there was going to be a tea party. Thought you could use rescuing," she whispered.

How had she heard that? Had my mom talked to hers? Not that it mattered. She was as welcome as a Saint Bernard, following an avalanche.

She peered around me into the hallway. "Hi, Ms. Sneaux."

"Would you like to join us for tea?" Mom asked.

"Uh, no, actually, the guys are playing volleyball. I thought Ashleigh would like to watch. Is that okay?"

"Of course," Mom said. "Y'all go have fun."

"Thanks, Mom." I gave her a quick hug before grabbing my parka from the hall closet. I pulled my knit cap down over my ears and put on my gloves as I followed Nathalie outside.

"Thanks so much," I said. "We were making finger sandwiches."

She laughed. "Wait until your mom decides to have a tea tasting."

We went down the steps. "Excuse me? A tea tasting?"

"Yeah, it's like a wine tasting, except you serve tea."

"Don't you have to make each type of tea in a different teapot?"

"I guess."

I couldn't think of anything that would be more boring.

"Wait until you see my boyfriend play," Nathalie said as we crossed the street. "He's really athletic." She bumped up against me. "And hot. Quite honestly, he's the hottest guy on the island."

Someone hotter than Chase and Josh? I couldn't wait to see this guy. I wondered if some sort of mutant gene had developed on the island that made all the guys good-looking. I mean, really, what were the odds that there wouldn't be any dorks around here? Let's hear it for gene mutation.

We went over the knoll and down toward the beach. I could see some guys on either side of the net, playing very seriously. None of them were wearing coats. I wondered which one was Nathalie's boyfriend. With the exception of a boy who looked like he was about twelve, they were all boyfriend-worthy.

Chase, Josh, and two guys I didn't know were on one side of the net. Not only were they not wearing coats, they weren't wearing shirts, either!

How insane was that?

"They have to be freezing!" I said, trying not to

notice how buff Josh looked. But it was a little difficult to miss.

And it made sense that he would be totally in shape. Construction work required a lot of heavy lifting. I already knew he was strong. I just didn't think he'd look *that* great.

Chase wasn't bad, either. Stirring fudge was apparently excellent exercise.

I felt a tad guilty that my attention kept going back to Josh.

"It's too hard to play in coats and gloves," Nathalie said. "The games don't last long."

No kidding.

Corey and Shanna stood nearby, and we joined them.

"Still not used to the cold?" Corey asked me.

She was holding another coat in her arms. I thought about asking if I could borrow it. It was colder on the beach, because a breeze was blowing off the water.

"I don't know if I'll ever get used to it," I confessed. "Are you using that coat?"

She laughed. "It's Chase's. I'm being a good sister, so it won't be covered in snow when he's finished playing."

"Is your boyfriend playing?"

"Oh, yeah." She pointed to a guy on the other

team wearing a red sweatshirt with the sleeves cut off. "That's Adam. I'd be holding his coat, except he didn't bring one. And that guy"—she pointed toward a guy who was at least wearing a long-sleeve T-shirt—"is Rand, Shanna's boyfriend."

"Are there many guys without girlfriends?" I asked.

"Nope. Just Chase and—"

"Watch out!" someone yelled.

A volleyball came soaring at us. I ducked. The girls laughed.

"Their hands get so cold they can't control where they hit the ball," Nathalie said.

"Isn't there someplace where they could play inside?" I asked.

"What would be the fun in that?" Shanna asked.

But the way the guys were shivering, I wasn't certain this method was much fun either.

I turned back to Corey, so she could finish giving me the official list of girlfriendless guys, but her cell phone rang and she moved away to answer it.

I thought about asking Shanna or Nathalie but I didn't want to appear to be obsessing about getting a boyfriend. I mean, I didn't want a boyfriend. I was just trying to figure out how many dates I could have before I ran through the menu. Chase. Maybe Josh. I knew he didn't have a girlfriend. Otherwise, he wouldn't have invited me to come watch him play. I hadn't considered that Chase would be here. I hoped it wouldn't get awkward after the game. I probably should have mentioned to Josh that I had a date with Chase.

Josh hit the ball over the net. Another guy slapped it back at him.

"My boyfriend is so good," Nathalie said. "I love watching him."

So the other guy was her boyfriend. He was okay-looking, not what I'd call the hottest guy on the island. But of course, Nathalie would think that about her boyfriend.

It suddenly occurred to me that she always referred to him as "my boyfriend." Like he was a thing, a status symbol. Maybe he was in this small community, where there weren't many guys to choose from.

"Game point!" Chase yelled.

He served the ball. The wind off the cold lake caught it and sent it out of bounds.

All the guys groaned. The one who looked like he was about twelve ran over, grabbed the ball, and threw it to Chase. He adjusted where he stood, tried again, and got it inbounds. After a couple of volleys, it went to Josh. He spiked it.

No one was able to move fast enough to return it. I was surprised they could move at all.

"Game!" Chase yelled.

"My boyfriend needs warming," Nathalie cried, and she ran toward the players, unzipping her jacket.

Josh turned. He saw me. He grinned. I grinned back, raised my hand—

Nathalie leaped at him, her coat opened wide. Slipping his arms around her, beneath the coat, he lifted her up and kissed her.

8

Okaayyy . . . I had not expected that.

I tried not to look surprised, shocked, stunned. But the truth was, I was all three. And maybe even a little hurt.

I remembered Nathalie saying that her boyfriend could paint my room. Oh, yeah. He could do a lot of things. He was a handyman.

"I could use some warming," a deep voice said.

I tore my gaze from the couple playing tonsil hockey. Chase was grinning at me like a fool.

"That's what coats are for," Corey said, shoving the heavy coat she'd been holding into his arms.

"That's not as much fun," he said, but he put the coat on anyway.

"Come on, everyone, let's go!" Nathalie shouted.

She was walking toward us awkwardly, since Josh's arm was around her, keeping her anchored to his side. He'd thrown on a bulky sweater and a jacket that he hadn't bothered to zip.

"Where are we going?" I asked.

"To my house, to get some hot apple cider and warm up these guys," Nathalie said.

Josh gave me an odd look as he walked by with Nathalie. The old furrowed brow, like he was trying to figure me out. What was to figure out? Other than why he hadn't told me he had a girlfriend.

"You're coming, right?" Chase asked.

"Oh, sure."

He walked beside me as we trudged toward Nathalie's house.

"I hear you've been hanging out with my sister," he said.

"Not really hanging out. We went to the mall together."

"Like I said, hanging out. Don't take anything she might say about me seriously, though, okay?"

"You mean I shouldn't take it seriously when she said you're the best brother in the whole world?"

"If she said that, then we've both dropped into an alternate universe. She's more likely to tell you to steer clear of me. We have this whole sibling rivalry thing."

"But she was holding your coat."

"Yeah, but I paid her to do it. So you have any sisters or brothers?"

"Nope."

"Yeah, neither does Nathalie," he said. "I think she gets lonely. I think it's one of the reasons she hooked up with a boyfriend so fast, before anyone else had a chance to audition for the role."

It seemed an odd thing to say, until I realized that he was watching her back, more than he was watching anything else. I briefly wondered if his asking me out was to make her jealous.

Up ahead, Nathalie laughed. Josh looked down at her and gave her a quick kiss.

I was beginning to wish I'd stayed at home making finger sandwiches.

Nathalie's house was warm and cozy, but still I kept my cap and coat on. I didn't plan to stay long. I did finally remove my gloves, but only because I wanted to wrap my bare hands around a warm mug of apple cider. I'd never had apple cider that tasted like maple syrup. Nathalie had dropped a blob of spiced butter into it. Standing at the edge of the kitchen, with my hip pressed to the counter, I stared at the melting butter, wishing I could disappear as easily.

All these people knew one another. They were laughing and talking about things that didn't include me, like the first time Josh ever dared to play snow volleyball sans shirt, and the guys on the other team had tossed him into a snow bank.

Laugh, laugh, laugh.

Or the time that old Mrs. Hooper—whoever the heck she was—paid Josh and Chase to clear her attic of bats.

Or how when a group of tourists came over for the day and . . .

Ha! Ha! Ha!

All I could do was smile, nod, and pretend I knew what they were talking about.

Finally, I got tired of listening and backed into the living room. A fire was crackling in the fireplace. My hands were still cold so I walked over to it and knelt. I put my mug on the floor and put my hands near the dancing flames. The wood-burning fire generated a lot of heat. It felt really good and smelled even better.

I knew log fires were a lot of trouble, but I wondered if Mom would consider converting our gas fireplaces to wood-burning ones, for the atmosphere . . . and the warmth.

I was so absorbed that I didn't know anyone was near until I heard knees pop. Josh crouched beside me.

"You okay?" he asked.

"Sure, why wouldn't I be?" I didn't look at him. I was pretending to be dazzled by the fire, because I didn't want him to see the lie in my eyes.

"I don't know. You just looked . . . surprised out there when . . . uh . . . Nathalie and I . . . you know."

Where had the smooth-talking lumberjack gone? He seemed to be as awkward as I felt.

"You never said you had a girlfriend, so yeah, I was a *little* surprised."

I couldn't bring myself to be totally honest about how it had stunned me, because he might correctly read that I was beginning to have an interest in him that went beyond painting walls.

"But you and Nathalie are friends. Didn't she tell—"

"That she had a boyfriend, yeah, but she never told me who he was." I did look at him then. He looked as confused as I probably had out at the volleyball net.

"So, what? She never mentioned me by name?"

"Right. She just said 'my boyfriend.' My boyfriend this. My boyfriend that. My boyfriend, my boyfriend, my boyfriend."

He furrowed his brow deeply. "Huh."

"Yeah," I said. I almost added that it was like he

was a trophy, but I had a feeling he was already thinking that.

"So, when you and I were talking . . . you didn't think I was coming on to you, did you?"

"Oh, no, of course not," I lied.

He seemed to think about that.

"I was just being friendly," he finally said.

"Me too. Totally."

"I mean, I have a girlfriend."

"Which I now know."

"What if I didn't?"

I went completely still. Not even breathing. I seemed to do that a lot when he was around. "What if you didn't what?"

"Would it make a difference if I didn't have a girlfriend?"

"I don't believe in playing what-if games."

"It's not a game."

"It's not reality, either."

He narrowed his eyes.

"Hey, you two," Nathalie said, dropping down to the floor so she was sorta wedged between us, and almost sitting in Josh's lap. "What are you doing?"

"Just trying to get warm," Josh and I said at the same time.

Weird. Great minds and all that. So if we both

thought alike, why didn't I realize he had a girlfriend? Why hadn't he figured out that I didn't know? And why hadn't Nathalie ever said anything? She had to know he was working at my house.

Nathalie took Josh's hand and began rubbing it. "His hands stay cold for so long after he plays volleyball. It's insane, isn't it? That the guys play winter volleyball half dressed?"

"Totally," I agreed.

"Have you ever seen anything like it?"

"Nope. This much snow and this much cold is a totally new experience."

"You know what? You should go cross-country skiing with us tomorrow. It's the best way to get up close and personal with the island." She rubbed her shoulder against Josh's. "That would be okay, wouldn't it? To have Ashleigh come along?"

"Sure," Josh said with as much enthusiasm as a senior being told he was being demoted to freshman.

"I've never skied," I said, trying to find a diplomatic way to say no-way-no-how was I going on an outing with Nathalie and "her boyfriend."

"Oh, it's easy," Nathalie assured me. "Toddlers can do it. You can use Chase's skis. He lives next door, so it won't be a problem to get them, and he's working at the fudge shop tomorrow, so he won't need them."

"I don't want to butt in . . ."

She snuggled against Josh. "No problem. Think of us as the welcome committee. Really, it'll be loads of fun."

Before I could offer another protest, Chase dropped down beside me. "Hey, what's going on here?"

"Just getting warm," I said.

"Ashleigh's going cross-country skiing with me and Josh tomorrow. She's going to use your skis."

"And what if I want to use them?" Chase asked.

"You're working. You can't use them."

"That's okay," I said. "If you don't want—"

"It's fine," Chase said. "You can use them. We'll work out payment Friday night. We're still going out, right?"

"You two are going out?" Josh asked before I could respond.

"Yeah," Chase said. "Is that a problem?"

"Not at all. I just didn't realize—"

"No reason you should, dude. I don't run my social calendar by you."

Was I sensing a little tension here?

"I'll walk you home," Chase said to me.

"You don't have to do that," I said.

"It's no trouble."

"All right." I pushed myself to my feet.

"So my boyfriend and I will see you tomorrow, right after lunch," Nathalie said.

I almost asked if she knew her boyfriend had a name, and if she knew what it was.

Josh looked at her funny, like maybe he was just realizing that she had this strange habit of never, and I do mean never, referring to him by name.

"Sounds good," I said.

"Hey, are you guys leaving?" Shanna asked. Before we could answer, she added, "Don't forget the hayride Thursday night. We'll be by to pick up everyone around seven. Are you in, Ashleigh?"

"Yeah, she's in," Chase said, winking at me.

"Guess I'm in."

Everything was happening so fast, just when I was getting used to everything happening so slowly.

I bundled myself up and followed Chase outside. I'd forgotten how cold it was. Especially when we turned the corner and the wind from off the lake hit us. I was thinking that buying fur-lined boots wasn't enough. Finding some fur-lined underwear might not be a bad idea.

"Was something going on between you and Josh back there?" I finally asked.

Chase gave me a crooked smile. "Nah. Not really. Just . . . you know."

Actually I didn't know, which was why I'd asked. But it seemed rude to pester him about something he obviously didn't want to talk about.

"I mean, couples hook up when they're kids, and then no one else gets a chance to date," he said. "That's all."

Was he saying that he wanted to date Nathalie?

"But you didn't hook up with anyone. I thought it was because you like fudgies."

He shrugged. "That's what Nathalie thinks."

Did that mean it wasn't true?

"So, what do you think of island life so far?" he asked. I guess he could see that I was trying to figure out what he was really saying—and he didn't want me thinking about it.

"Love the fudge," I said, grinning.

He grinned back. "Yeah, it's hard to beat."

"Everything seems to move slower here."

"You should see it during the summer."

"Do things speed up then?"

"No, not really, but you can find more things to do. Horseback riding. Bicycling. Hiking. Lots of good hiking trails and caves to explore."

"I guess there's more to this island than I realized. So about this hayride . . ."

"Shanna's dad owns one of the freight companies, so they have these big old wagons. Every year they load hay onto a couple of them, and we ride over the island, stopping at houses along the way for apple cider. It's fun. Did you not want to do it?"

"Oh, no, I'd love to. It sounds like a lot of fun."

"Great. And don't worry. We haven't even had our date yet, so we won't kiss if you don't want to."

I released a slight laugh. "Excuse me, but this city girl has never been on a hayride. Is there something special I need to know?"

He grinned. "Hayrides are good for kissing. A natural way to keep warm."

"Ah, I see."

He held up his hands. "But like I said, no pressure."

"Thanks . . . I think."

We arrived at Chateau Ashleigh.

"Thanks for walking me home," I said.

"Sure. I'll see you Thursday."

He walked off. And I went inside.

Mom was in the parlor, curled up on the couch, in front of the fire. She smiled at me. "Have fun?"

"Oh, yeah."

On Mom's lap was her *Teatime* book. A couple of Post-its were sticking out of it. I guess she'd tried some more sandwiches while I was gone.

"I'm going cross-country skiing tomorrow," I told her. "With Nathalie and her boyfriend."

Didn't that sound exciting?

"You don't ski."

"Apparently it's not that hard." I sat in the chair, pulled off my boots, and brought my feet up underneath me. "I've been thinking, Mom. There are a lot of bed-and-breakfasts on this island. Why don't we open a dinner-then-bed inn? You know, something different, something that doesn't require getting up early?"

She gave me a look and said, "Nice try."

"So he had a girlfriend this whole time?" Tara asked later, when I called her.

"Yeah."

"And he never said anything?"

"Nope."

"Jerk."

I don't know why I grimaced at her harsh tone. What did I care if she liked Josh or not? I didn't. Still, I felt compelled to say, "He thought I knew."

"But he never talked about her. How much can

he like her if he never talks about her?"

Tara was no doubt basing that opinion on the fact that she talked about Shaun all the time.

"It's not like we're best buds," I mumbled.

"But he should have said something! Especially since he knew you knew her."

"It doesn't matter."

"You were really starting to like him," she said.

"No, not really." Okay, I really was. I mean, the whole encounter on the ladder had gotten to me, but I didn't want to talk about it anymore. To change the subject, I said, "So how are things with Shaun?"

"Things are great. We've actually been talking about coming up there to spend some time before winter break is over. Think your mom would give us a special on two rooms?"

"Hey, for you the rooms would be free."

"Seriously?"

"Oh, yeah. I mean, we're not even set up yet to register guests. Mom and I wouldn't even know where to start."

"So when would be a good time to come?"

"Are you serious?"

"I think so. I'll double-check with Shaun. I *think* he was excited about the idea, but you know sometimes it's hard to tell with him if he's really excited."

I did know.

"That would be awesome if y'all would come."

"Yeah, it would be. I miss you, Ash."

"Not as much as I miss you. It's really, really different here."

And that was, quite possibly, the understatement of the year.

"So what are you going to do about Josh?"

Tara could be sidetracked for only so long.

"I don't know. I have to think—"

"Oh, sorry. Shaun's here. I've gotta run. I'll call you later."

Only I knew she wouldn't. Because with Shaun there, later would be really late. So it was left to me and me alone to figure out how I was going to get out of going cross-country skiing with Nathalie and her boyfriend tomorrow.

The truth was I didn't want to see Nathalie hanging all over Josh. Because, yeah, Tara was right. I had really started to like him.

9

"Are you ready?"

I was standing on the ladder, working on the stenciling. I had been all morning. It was something to do. Unfortunately, it was a brainless activity, so I'd had way too much time to think about my afternoon plans.

Josh had been in the room next door most of the morning, moving furniture around, covering it up, and removing the old wallpaper before putting up the new. Or at least, that's what I assumed he was doing. I'd heard a lot of banging, bumping, and scraping going on.

But this was the first time that we'd actually spoken to each other that morning. He was standing in the doorway now, jacket on but unbuttoned, as usual.

"Listen, you go on ahead. I want to finish this up," I said with a casual wave toward the stencil. Purple tulips.

"You've got a few more hours' worth."

"Yeah, I know."

"Nathalie's expecting us."

"Like I said, go ahead. You and her. Go have your time together."

"She wanted to share the island with you."

"Yeah, well, it's always awkward being the odd number in a group."

"So I'll be the odd number."

I just stared at him. Did he not get what I was saying?

"How can you be the odd number?" I asked.

"Two girls, one guy. It even makes more sense for me to be the odd one."

"Except you and Nathalie will be all snugly—"

"It's a little awkward to snuggle on skis. Besides, I packed enough food for all of us."

"Excuse me?"

"Lunch. I brought lunch. Oh, and be sure to wear good hiking boots. I want to show you something special, and we'll need to hike there."

He turned and disappeared from the doorway.

"Hey, wait! Come back! I really don't want to go!"

Only, he didn't wait, he didn't come back, and

I still really didn't want to go.

Well, okay, maybe I did a little. I mean, cross-country skiing did sound like something that would be fun, exciting even. I did want to make the most of the winter. And Josh had offered to show me something special, which of course piqued my curiosity. Although I couldn't admit that to him, or even to myself.

Because I could have no interest in him whatsoever. He was officially off-limits as dating material.

I scrambled down the ladder and hurried to my room where I put on layers of clothing: a T-shirt, a Henley knit top, a thick sweater, a parka, jeans, two pairs of socks, and yes, my hiking boots.

Josh was waiting for me by the door, a huge backpack at his feet. "I already told your mom that we were heading out."

"What made you so sure I'd show?"

"The something special."

"What is it, exactly?"

"You'll see."

He shrugged into his backpack. When we got outside, he lifted a pair of skis that he'd obviously set there earlier.

It took us less than five minutes to get to Nathalie's. Only when she came to the door, she wasn't dressed for hiking. She was still in her PJ's, holding a Kleenex to her nose. "Sorry, guys," she said with a raspy voice, "but I'm miserable. Go on without me."

"We can't do that," I said. "This was your idea."

"It's okay, really." She sniffed. "And I've been before." She coughed. "You can use my skis." She pointed toward the corner of the porch, where some skis were set. "Have fun."

She closed the door.

Until that moment I hadn't realized that being a third wheel was sometimes better than being the second wheel. Josh and I stood there, both stumped as to what to do next.

He finally cleared his throat. "Well, huh."

"Yeah," I said. "What now?"

"Well"—he cleared his throat again—"I guess you and I go. I mean, unless you really don't want to."

Why put it on me to bail out?

"Do you want to?" I asked.

"Yeah. I really do. I had to talk Dad into giving me the afternoon off. And since I don't usually go to a lot of trouble to fix lunch, it seems a shame to waste the effort. Besides, there's the thing I want you to see."

He said all of this while staring at the door like

he was talking to it. I almost expected it to respond.

"Okay, sure," I said, doing a perfect emotionless imitation of Shaun of the Dead.

I edged past him and picked up the skis.

"I'll carry those," he said.

We walked up the street a ways and then he took a turn down another street. My breath was visible, and I concentrated on it, breathing through my mouth, trying to form smoke rings. It didn't really work.

"Are you mad at me or something?" Josh asked after a while.

"No, not mad."

"But you're something," he said.

"Yeah, *something*."

"Are you gonna make me guess what it is?"

I thought about it. Sighed. Decided to tell him what was bugging me.

"You could have mentioned you had a girlfriend."

"You could have mentioned you had a date with Chase."

"Why would I mention that?"

"Why would I mention that I had a girlfriend?"

I stopped dead in my tracks. "Uh, maybe because having a girlfriend is a big deal, and maybe

I had the impression you liked me—"

He spun around and faced me. I swallowed hard. He looked angrier than I was.

"Like I said, I thought you knew," he ground out.

"Well, I didn't."

"But you still made plans to go out with Chase, so whether or not I had a girlfriend didn't really seem to be an issue for you."

"When he asked I didn't even know you! So, what? I'm supposed to cancel my date with him when I meet you? Or say to you when we met, 'Hey, guess what? I have a date!' Why would I even think you'd care?"

"Same goes! When exactly was I supposed to announce that I had a girlfriend? When we were discussing paint?"

"I don't know. It just seems like there was a moment, *some*time, when you could have said—"

"Well, there wasn't, so get over it."

"Okay, then." I clapped my gloved hands in front of his face. They didn't make a sound nearly as loud as I wanted. "I'm over it."

"Great."

"Yeah, great." It just didn't feel great. "So what are we doing here?" I asked.

"We're going cross-country skiing, and I'm

going to show you something."

"Could you be any more enthusiastic about it?"

He released a deep breath that would have fogged all the windows in my dad's Hummer.

"Okay, look," he said. "I mean, I've got a girl-friend, you have a date, but we can still be friends, right?"

Could we? I'd been friends with lots of guys. Dated lots of guys. Even if he didn't have a girl-friend, I'd only go out with him a time or two . . . okay, maybe three times. All right, maybe four. Four tops. But he did have a girlfriend. So he wasn't dateable, but I did like him.

I nodded. "Yeah, okay. We can be friends."

"Friends share things. This thing I want to show you is really neat. You're gonna love it. And like I said, I went to a lot of trouble to fix lunch. So let's go enjoy ourselves."

"Okay." I could do that. I could force myself to have fun.

He jerked his head to the side. "Let's go then. We're burning daylight. Isn't that what they say in Texas?"

"Not anyone I know."

After a while we left the road. Josh climbed up a snowy embankment and reached back for me.

While I was wearing gloves, he wasn't. I could feel the strength in his hand as he pulled me up. I really didn't want to notice how strong he was. Or how big his hand was. Or that it was probably warm and I wouldn't mind feeling it against my cheek.

I guess we were officially in the natural part of the island, no longer the town. We were surrounded by leafless trees, occasional evergreens, and lots and lots of snow. I didn't know how anything survived here, but I'd seen pictures of the island in summertime and it was lush and green. So survival definitely happened.

And while I found this much snow a little disorienting, I had to admit that I found it beautiful as well.

"I sorta hate to ruin this by trampling through it," I said.

"People do it all the time. If you look around, you'll see other tracks. Besides, more snow will eventually fall to cover it up."

"You know, where I used to live we might have one day, maybe two, of snow all winter. If that. And most of the time, it stayed on the ground only a couple of hours. Some years it never snows. And it never stays looking this pretty. I've never known a winter like this."

"Never known a Wynter like me, either, I bet."

His eyes were sparkling and I laughed. "No, I never have."

All the awkwardness or irritation or whatever it was that had settled in between us seemed to melt away.

He showed me how to put on the skis, with the toe jammed into place, the heel free. Then he demonstrated the sliding motion of cross-country skiing. Even with the ski poles, I found it hard to keep my balance. Josh grabbed me when I almost toppled—twice. To his credit, he didn't laugh either time.

When he thought I had the hang of it, he led the way toward wherever it was we were going.

A small part of me—okay, a large part—was glad that it was just the two of us. Not that I wanted Nathalie to be sick. It was just that I'd really started to like Josh. I was comfortable around him. And I liked watching the way he moved through the woods.

Every now and then he'd stop and wait for me to catch up.

"Just take your time; we're not racing," he said when I arrived nearly breathless. "You'll be sore tomorrow."

"You're not even breathing hard," I said, unable to keep the irritation out of my voice.

"I do this a lot. A few times a week. It's great exercise."

"You like the outdoors?"

"Oh, yeah. Come on. It's not that much farther."

I nodded, determined to tough it out. I wasn't quite as cold anymore. As a matter of fact, I was getting warm and was considering shedding a layer or two.

And I was glad that we weren't racing, because it gave me a chance to appreciate the tranquility of our surroundings.

We passed an old military cemetery, marked by an arch above the gate. The spikes of the picket fence were visible, but very few headstones were.

"I know this is probably weird," I called out to Josh, "but I like walking through old cemeteries."

He turned to face me. "It's not weird at all, but it would be kinda hard to walk through there today."

I nodded. "In the spring, maybe. I'll still be here."

"We can hike here then. We're actually on a pretty clearly marked trail. It's just not real obvious now because of all the snow, but it's easy to get here."

"I like reading old headstones."

"Some of the ones in there are really old, like

from when Britain and the colonies were at war. Not all the graves are clearly marked anymore."

"So you don't know who's buried there?"

"Not really."

"That's sad."

"The Preservation Society puts flags on the graves on Memorial Day."

"Everyone here is into history, huh?"

"Pretty much." He jerked his thumb over his shoulder. "It's not too much farther. We'll eat first."

"You went to a lot of trouble for *this*?" I asked incredulously.

We were sitting on a covered stone picnic table near a natural stone arch. Through it, we had a beautiful view of the lake.

Josh had put a folded quilt on top of the table, which we were sitting on since, even with the overhead covering, snow had managed to find its way in and was piled around the bench seats. And even with the quilted padding beneath us, my butt was still cold. Although after our trek over the snow, the rest of me was actually kind of warm.

I held up the pre-packaged pimento cheese sandwich and repeated, "For *this*?"

Josh grinned and tossed a bag of sour cream and onion chips into my lap. "I didn't say it was anything elaborate."

"You gave the impression it was something you'd *cooked yourself.*"

"I put a lot of thought into which items to buy."

Laughing, I shook my head. Did he seriously think that counted?

He pulled out a Thermos, poured hot chocolate into the mug-shaped top, and handed it to me. It was warm and really good.

"You redeemed yourself," I told him.

"Even better than that." He took out a bag of miniature marshmallows. He scooped out a few and dropped them in the mug.

I watched the steam rise, thinking that a guy who went to the trouble to bring not only hot chocolate but marshmallows really was something special.

I'd never been one to envy a girl because of her boyfriend. But right now I was sorta thinking that Nathalie had it really good.

Not that I should have been thinking about Josh at all, or comparing him to anyone, or envying the girl he'd hooked up with.

So I went straight to a topic that was totally boring but would at least stop me from thinking about how much I liked sitting in the cold with

Josh. I didn't want to even think about how much more I'd like it in the summer.

"I'm used to lazy picnics," I said. "But I'm guessing we're not going to dawdle here, are we?"

"Not really. There's a limestone cavern over there that I want to show you."

"Is it safe?"

"No, Ash, it's incredibly dangerous. That's the reason I want to eat first. In case it's our last meal."

I decided to totally ignore the fact that he called me Ash, which only my best friends did.

"You want your last meal to be pimento cheese?"

He grinned. "Nah, I'd want it to be steak. So I guess we'd better survive."

He took the mug from me, gulping down a good deal of the hot chocolate and the marshmallows that were melting on top. It felt like a really intimate thing to do—sharing the mug—but I understood his not wanting to weigh his backpack down with a bunch of mugs.

He poured more hot chocolate and dropped more marshmallows into the mug before handing it back.

"Thanks," I said. "So you must do this a lot. You seem to have the routine down."

"Whether I'm hiking or skiing I always get

hungry, so yeah, I always make sure I bring something to eat." He dug into his backpack and brought out a package of cupcakes. Since he wasn't wearing gloves, I was surprised he had enough dexterity left in his cold hands to open it and hand me one.

"You're not really into home cooking, are you?" I asked.

"No. Are you?"

I shook my head. "Mom nixed the bed-and-dinner idea, by the way—for that very reason. Dinner is way more complicated to cook than breakfast."

Grinning, he shook his head. "Guess you could always hire someone to cook breakfast."

"Now that's an idea." I bit into the cupcake and chewed. "I don't guess y'all have a school football team."

He gave me a really broad grin. "I can't believe you really say *y'all*."

"Well, I do. Football?"

"No team. Football is really big in Texas, isn't it?"

"Everything is really big in Texas, but yeah, football is king."

"Seemed like it in *Friday Night Lights*."

"You bet. So are there any athletics here at all?"

"Sure. We're not the only island around here.

Plus some nearby harbor towns have small schools, too. We play in the Northern Lights League—soccer, baseball, and volleyball."

"Are you on any of the teams?"

"I'm on all of them. How 'bout you? You play any sports?"

"No, but I'm big into going to games."

"That's great. We can use all the cheering fans we can get."

I took a sip of the hot chocolate, feeling the warm mist tickle my nose for a millisecond before it cooled. "I have to confess, I'm a little nervous about going to such a small school."

"*Big* schools in Texas?"

"Not all of them," I said. "But mine is . . . was. Whatever. Anyway, we had over a thousand kids in my class."

He shook his head. "See, I don't know if I'd like that. You could get lost with a school that big."

"But a school so small . . ."

"I think you'll like it. Everyone knows everyone."

"It's gonna be weird."

"But you'll adjust. I mean, look how well you're adjusting to snow. No one would guess you'd never cross-country skied before."

"Yeah, right." I didn't bother to hide my skepticism.

The cold was seriously seeping through the quilt onto my butt, and a shudder went through me. I downed the rest of the lukewarm chocolate. Nothing around here stayed heated for long.

"So where is this cavern, and why would I want to see it?" I asked.

"Because you have a thing for rodents."

"I like cute little mice—Disney mice. Rodents, rats, no."

"We'll see," he said and shoved himself off the table.

"You know, live rodents, they just don't appeal to me," I emphasized.

"Trust me. These will."

10

We climbed up a short embankment, leaving our skis and backpack at the bottom. Josh carried a large flashlight. That was reassuring. I'd been in caves before, but always with a tour guide or a clearly marked path.

I was amazed to see a dark gaping hole in the side of the knoll or hill or whatever it was officially called. I wasn't exactly on a first-name basis with nature.

"I'm surprised it's not covered up with snow," I said. Although maybe it had been and a bear had shoved his way out. Did bears live on this island?

"It was this morning," Josh said. "I came earlier to check it out and make sure it was safe."

"Good to know we were never in danger of pimento cheese being our last meal."

I glanced around. We were totally alone. Not a soul in sight.

"Should we be doing this?" I asked.

"Of course not, but that's never stopped me before." He switched on the flashlight and walked to the entrance of the cavern. "Come on."

He crawled inside. My survival instincts told me to stay exactly where I was, but I was curious. Besides, two fools were probably better than one. If he got into some sort of trouble in there, he'd need me to help get him out.

I crept in after him. It smelled dank and it felt like being inside a freezer. It was also very slippery, like walking on a thin layer of ice.

I could see Josh up ahead, the beam from the flashlight creating wavering light over the glistening walls. Suddenly he stopped and turned, directing the light toward me and holding out his hand.

It was so dark, except for where the flashlight directed its light, that I had a *Blair Witch Project* moment. What was I getting myself into?

I cautiously moved forward and put my hand in his. He pulled me through the opening. We entered a space just large enough that we could stand upright.

"There," he whispered, pointing the flashlight toward the ceiling, which was only inches above our head.

As a carpenter, maybe he was into studying nature's various architectural wonders. This ceiling, though, looked strange, uneven . . .

"Are those—?"

"Bats," he said in a low voice, but he sounded triumphant.

While I was trying to decide whether to be amazed or terrified, I settled for being put out. "Bats are not rodents."

"I know, but don't they look like mice with wings? Pretty cool, huh?"

"Unless they wake up, swoop down, and attack us. Don't they carry rabies?"

"That's an old wives' tale," he said. "A very miniscule percentage actually have rabies. Watch this."

Reaching up, he unhooked a bat from its perch.

"Are you insane?" I whispered.

"Shh. It's okay. They're hibernating." He hung it on the sleeve of his jacket and held it up to my face. "Is that awesome or what?"

It *was* kinda awesome. I'd never seen a bat up close like this.

"Go ahead and pet it," he said.

It looked pretty harmless. I reached out—

It released an ear-splitting screech and flew toward me!

I let loose a blood-curdling scream and found

myself facedown on the floor of the cave, with Josh lying on top of me, covering me, while the cave filled with the horrendous echoing of a thousand angry wings.

When things finally quieted, we scrambled out of the cave, sliding down the snowy embankment until we landed on even ground.

I was breathless, my heart beating so hard that I figured it would wake up *all* the hibernating creatures within a five-mile radius.

Laughing, Josh dropped back in the snow, like he was planning to make a snow angel or something. But I figured that was the last thing on his mind.

"They've never done that before. Scared the crap out of me," he said.

I figured I'd just scared ten years off my life expectancy. I was shaking, and it wasn't from the cold.

We were both breathing hard. I had my arms wrapped around my drawn-up knees, trying to be as small and unnoticeable as possible. I pressed my forehead to my legs. "Do you go in there a lot?"

"Yeah. I like studying bats. Weird, I know—"

"No, not weird." I glanced over at him. "My grandparents live in Austin. I've seen bats there when I've gone to visit them. I think it's neat to watch them. And when we went on vacation at Carlsbad, my dad and I watched the bats leaving the cavern at sunset, then we got up before dawn to watch them coming back. It was totally awesome, the way they just swooped in one after another."

He didn't say anything for a moment, just looked at me. Maybe he was trying to figure out why I thought he'd care about my previous bat-seeking excursions.

"I should have told you I had a girlfriend," he said quietly.

He shoved himself into a sitting position. "I really did think that Nathalie had told you, but I didn't say anything because if she hadn't—or even if she had—I didn't want to talk about her. I just wanted to find out everything I could about you. I wanted to get to know you. And I guess I felt kinda guilty about that."

My breathing had slowed. As a matter of fact, it had almost stopped completely. Because while he'd talked he'd moved really close to me. I could see the deep blue of his eyes.

"I like you a lot, Ash."

Our breaths were visible as they mingled, intertwined.

"A whole lot," he said in a low voice.

Then our breaths were no longer mingling, because neither of us was breathing. We were kissing.

And all I could think about was how much I liked the swirl, that Josh was an absolute master at kissing.

I had a feeling the snow around us was going to start melting.

But as much as I enjoyed him kissing me, as much as I didn't want him to stop, I couldn't help wondering . . .

Had I just become the other woman?

11

I shoved Josh's shoulder, breaking us apart.

"We can't do this," I said, scrambling away from him, getting to my feet. "You've got a girl-friend."

"Don't you think I know that?"

"Based on the past couple of minutes, I'd say you forgot."

"Ash, wait!"

I was skidding onto the trail, desperate to get to the skis, trying to figure out how I could move the quickest—by ski or by foot.

He grabbed my arm. I jerked free. "Don't! Nathalie was my first friend here. I'm not going to do *that* to her," I said, pointing back to the place where we'd been kissing. The snow was no longer pristine there. It had obviously been disturbed.

"Look, I'm sorry, I've just wanted to kiss you ever since that first morning—"

I shoved him hard, he staggered back. "That's the reason you didn't tell me you had a girlfriend. You were flirting with me."

"No. I mean, okay, maybe I didn't intentionally mention Nathalie because I thought you'd put up barriers. I know it makes me sound like a jerk, but I don't want to hurt Nathalie. I mean, she's been my girlfriend since I was twelve. I care about her."

"Oh, yeah, that was real obvious back there."

I jammed the toe of my boot into the ski, locked it in place, and reached for the other.

"I've never kissed another girl," he said.

"Yeah, right." I shoved the other boot into place.

"I swear, I never have. I've never done anything like that before. I've never wanted to."

"Then why me?" I spun around to face him, lost my balance, and landed on my butt.

He was beside me before I could blink.

"I don't know," he said quietly. "I honest to God don't know."

He wrapped his hand around my arm, helped me to my feet, or my skis, rather. Whatever. He helped me stand.

I was frazzled, upset. I didn't want to be the other woman—the other girl—the person who tore them apart, who might be responsible for . . .

Omigod! What if they broke up and it was my fault?

"That's never going to happen again," I said determinedly.

"Okay."

I heard the resignation in his voice.

"Okay," I said, hearing the disappointment in mine.

I watched him drop the flashlight into his backpack before shrugging it onto his shoulders. He put on his skis, concentrating on a task that I figured he could probably do in his sleep.

"I'm sorry," I said quietly. "But I can't be the other girl."

He glanced over at me and gave me a sad sort of smile. "I know."

"She's crazy about you."

He squeezed his eyes shut like the words hurt. He heaved a deep sigh. "We need to get back."

He started to move past me and I grabbed his arm. "And Josh, I don't do boyfriends."

"Okay, already. I get it." I heard the irritation in his voice. "Let's just go."

"No." Shaking my head, I held his gaze. "I didn't say that right. What I mean is that I don't want a boyfriend. I like to date, but I only go out with a guy a couple of times. I don't want anything permanent. I'm not like the girls here. They all have boyfriends. I don't want one."

"But Chase—"

"He likes to date around too. So we'll have some fun. Then he'll move on to the fudgies and I'll"—I sighed—"move on to online dating."

"And hook up with a serial killer?"

I wrinkled my nose, which was going numb with the cold. "Okay, the same thought occurred to me. But the point is, I shouldn't have gotten upset about you having a girlfriend, because the most you and I would have is a date or two."

I'd convinced myself that's the way it would be. I wasn't upset that he had a girlfriend. I was upset that we wouldn't have a single date.

"How do you know?" he asked. "You might really like me—"

"I don't do boyfriends. Period. No, exclamation mark."

"What are you afraid of?"

I scoffed. "Nothing. Just following my mom's advice."

"No one follows their mom's advice."

"Well, I do. And I just felt like I should let you know. Because I totally overreacted."

And I found some comfort in knowing that I wouldn't be faced with making a decision regarding our relationship.

"Okay," he said. "Let's go home."

I seemed to have finally learned how to move quickly and smoothly using the skis. I didn't lose my balance once. Before I knew it, we came out of the woods and onto the trail that would lead to the street.

We took off our skis and started walking.

Josh glanced over his shoulder. "A taxi's coming. Do you want to grab a ride? I'll pay."

I glanced back over my shoulder. This one was a sleigh instead of a wagon like we'd taken from the airport.

The reality was that I wanted nothing more than to take a sleigh ride with Josh. But only because I thought it would be romantic. And romance was the one thing I couldn't have with him.

"No. I'm good walking."

The horse clomped by, the runners sliding with ease over the snow-packed ground. Watching it disappear around the bend, I wondered if I'd ever take a romantic sleigh ride.

As we got nearer to Nathalie's, I said, "Thank Nathalie for letting me use her skis."

"You're not coming up to the house?"

"No, I think I'll go on." I don't know why, but I was afraid she'd see evidence in my face that I'd kissed her boyfriend. Like maybe he was branded on my lips or something. Silly, I know, but guilt can give you really weird thoughts.

"Well, thanks for going with me," he said.

"Yeah, sure." I stopped myself from saying, "Anytime."

Because the truth was, I really couldn't do this with him anytime. As a matter of fact, I could never do it again, because already I was wishing that we'd kissed a little longer, that I had a few more minutes of the memory.

"Thanks for sharing the bats with me," I said. "Even though they aren't rodents."

"It was sure an experience I'll never forget," he said.

I thought he might have been talking about more than the bats, but he didn't elaborate, and I was glad. I wanted to believe that the attraction had taken him completely by surprise and that he wasn't a jerk.

That he wasn't like my dad.

I loved my dad, but it hurt that he was marrying someone else. I tried so hard not to think about it.

Josh stopped at the fence in front of Nathalie's

house. I probably should have stopped too, but I kept going.

"I'll see you around," he called after me.

Not if I see you first.

A totally childish thing to think. Fortunately, I didn't give in to my instincts to say it. Instead, I gave him a wave and continued on, wishing I didn't know what it was like to spend time with him, to share moments with him, and most of all to kiss him.

12

I know some girls load up on ice cream when they're feeling blue. Others gorge on white chocolate chip macadamia nut cookies—preferably warm, with the chocolate still melted. Tara usually curls up with a romance novel that she sneaks out of the stash beneath her mom's bed.

But me? I indulge in horror movies.

Fortunately, our little section of the island had a video store, cleverly named Videos, Etc. Although it was already dark, I walked over. Apparently the crime rate here was zero. Back home no way would I have walked several blocks, alone in the dark. But it was different here. I felt totally safe.

The clerk behind the counter greeted me when I came in. He was tall and skinny. It seemed like every day was a bad hair day for him. His was sticking up at all angles, and obviously not due to any effort on his part.

The place was ominously quiet except for a Disney video playing on a small TV behind the counter.

The store was also noticeably absent of customers. I wasn't in any hurry, so I browsed the aisles looking for something different.

I could never get worked up about watching romantic movies. When Tara slept over, we always rented chick flicks—*Bridget Jones' Diary*, *Pride and Prejudice*. Tara has a real thing for English accents. We once did a twenty-four-hour marathon of chick flicks. They're fun when I'm watching them with someone who really enjoys watching them. But when it's just me . . . I like to be scared silly. Of course, my preference for scary movies over chick flicks made me a popular date. At least back home. I hadn't even seen a movie theater here.

I finally made it to the horror aisle, and much to my surprise, they had quite a selection. I heard a door open. The guy behind the counter issued his standard "hi," and a low voice answered back.

I crouched and picked up the case for *The Darkroom*. I hadn't seen it yet. My film selection of choice and my best friend were incompatible. When we did rent horror together, Tara had a habit of curling up in a chair with her eyes and ears covered for most of the movie. Where's the fun in that?

"You're kidding me. You like horror?"

I jerked my head around. Josh was standing there, studying me, acting like nothing had happened between us that afternoon. Like all was normal. I could pretend too.

"Uh . . ." I looked at the case I was holding, then looked at him. "As a matter of fact I do."

I stood up.

"Have you seen *The Ring*?" he asked.

"Opening day."

He leaned toward me and whispered low, "The little girl in that movie scared the crap out of me. I slept with my bedroom light on for a week."

"You should see *Ringu*. It's the Japanese version, and it's a lot scarier."

"You're into J-horror?" he asked.

Could he look any more surprised?

"Big-time."

Grinning, he looked me over, from the toes of my boots to the tassel on top of my knit cap. "You don't look the type."

"And what does *the type* look like, exactly?"

"Like someone who shaves."

"I shave."

"Not your face."

"What a sexist snob!"

He held up his hands like he was fending off an

attack. "I'm just saying . . . most girls I know watch horror movies with their eyes closed."

"What about Nathalie?"

That reminder—or maybe it was my sharp tone—knocked the grin off his face.

"Eyes totally closed," he said.

"I watch with mine wide open."

"I'm impressed. The next time a horror movie is showing around here, I might have to make you prove that."

Omigod! Had he just asked me out?

As if "Omigod! Did I just ask her out?" had suddenly flashed through his mind, his eyes widened and he suddenly became very interested in the movie selection.

"I haven't even seen a theater," I told him.

He kept his eyes on the videos. "One of the hotels has movie night every now and then in their ballroom."

"You're kidding."

No sixteen-screen multiplexes here. I shouldn't have been surprised, but I was.

He peered at me. "No. Plus there's a theater on the mainland."

He went back to studying the selections. I was about to head to the counter when he said, "Have you seen this one?" He held up *Jacob's Ladder*.

"Nope."

"I highly recommend it."

"Okay then." I took it from him and accepted his challenge, studying the various movies. "How 'bout . . . *Dark Water*?"

"Never seen it."

I handed it to him. "Exchanging DVDs. Does this mean we're going steady?"

Did I really say that? I didn't say that.

He laughed awkwardly and took another step back. "No, we're not . . . I mean, I'm already going steady with someone. And you don't *do* steady."

"Yeah, I know. I was kidding," I said quickly, then held up the DVD he'd given me like an old priest holding up a cross to ward off a vampire. "Thanks for the recommendation. Catch you later."

I walked to the counter where the "et cetera" part of the store was displayed. Candy bars, microwaveable packets of popcorn stuffed into tubs. Everything needed to provide a realistic movie-going experience.

Since I was a new customer, I had to fill out all the paperwork to be approved to rent a movie. I was almost finished when Josh came to the counter. When I turned to tell him to go ahead, I noticed one of the DVDs he was holding. I raised an eyebrow. "*Music and Lyrics?* You do realize that movie has a scare factor of zero."

He blushed. "Yeah, I know. Nathalie—"

"Enough said."

"She's feeling a little better."

"Good."

Suddenly I was no longer in the mood to let him cut in front of me. Petty, I know. But there you are. Unfortunately, the clerk didn't ask my opinion. He just went ahead and checked Josh out.

"Say hi to Nathalie," I said when he turned to leave.

"Will do."

He walked out the door.

After the paperwork was stamped "approved" and filed away, I paid for my rental. When I got outside, Josh was waiting with his back pressed against the wall.

He shoved himself away from the building. "I'll walk you home."

"I thought the streets were safe."

"From crime, sure, but what if you slip or twist your ankle? You're not exactly used to walking on snow and ice."

"I did okay this afternoon," I pointed out a little testily.

"Do you really want me to count how many

times I had to help you up or catch you before you fell?"

"Are you saying I'm a klutz?"

"Just saying . . ."

Of course, in one of those moments of irony, I—who had yet to slip when walking around this portion of the island—put my foot on some ice and, yes indeedy, my foot slid out from beneath me and I almost landed on my butt.

But Josh reached out, grabbed my arms, and pulled me close. Or as close as one bundled Eskimo—me—could get to a guy who obviously was never affected by cold. But even with all the comfy down stuffing between us, when my gloved hand pressed against his firm chest, I thought I could actually feel warmth seeping through his sweater into my skin.

"Point made," he said smugly, releasing me but making sure I remained steady.

"Not quite. Ankles are not twisted, sprained, or strained." Although I did feel a little twinge when I took a step, but no way was I going to admit that.

And I didn't think my limp was noticeable as we began walking down the street, another awkward silence stretching between us.

"So, I've been thinking," I began.

"Good hobby."

"Ha-ha."

I gave him a hard look. He grinned. I sighed. "Anyway, with no motorized vehicles around, do you even have a driver's license?"

"Sure. What kind of question is that?"

"How would you learn to drive?"

"Go to drivers' school on the mainland."

"It seems kinda pointless to get one. You can't drive anywhere."

"You know, we're not prisoners here. We can find lots of places to drive to on the mainland."

"Yeah, but you have no real experience. You'd be hazardous, a danger to other drivers."

"I'm a great driver. Not one ticket or accident."

"All guys think they're great drivers. Besides, the odds are in your favor, considering how seldom you drive—"

"Give me a break. I do a *lot* of driving."

I almost said something like, "Next time we're on the mainland you'll have to prove it." The problem was, it would give the impression we'd be going to the mainland together—which we never would. Ever. Besides, it bordered on that whole are-we-hinting-at-a-date thing again.

We came to an area where I could look through a large break between the buildings and see the bridge that joined the distant straits, connecting lower Michigan to the Upper Penninsula.

"The bridge is so pretty at night," I said.

"Yeah. There's nothing like it."

"Well, actually, we do have bridges in Texas."

"Yeah, I've heard about Texas. Everything is bigger there."

"Pretty much. I'll have to show you sometime."

Okay, so I fell into the date-comment trap. But it was just there, waiting to be used.

It's amazing how a quiet person can get even quieter when something is said that makes him start thinking. I needed him to stop thinking, to stop analyzing what I'd said. "I read somewhere that the strait freezes over," I blurted.

Why don't you just hold up a sign, Ash? Watch out! Changing topic up ahead!

"In another month or so, yeah," he said. "It's kinda cool really. We mark a trail with Christmas trees. Use it to cross the strait."

"On foot?"

"Sure. Or snowmobile. But I like walking."

I waited a heartbeat to see if he was going to say we'd walk together sometime. I was surprised when he didn't. Maybe even a little disappointed. I would have liked to have had one real date with him. Although this afternoon's experience could probably count.

It was difficult to stay angry or disappointed when the night surrounding us was so peaceful. The streetlights sent out a warm glow. The snow crunched slightly beneath our feet. A horse-drawn sleigh passed by us. The couple sitting inside was snuggled beneath a blanket.

"My friend Tara would love it here," I said. "She's a total romantic."

"She'd find the cold romantic?"

"No, doofus. The horse-drawn sleighs."

"What's romantic about them?"

I rolled my eyes. Guys. Honestly. "If you have to be told, then there's nothing romantic about them."

"They're transportation."

I wondered if a time would come when all the special things would no longer seem special to me.

We arrived at Chateau Ashleigh.

"Well, here we are. Thanks for keeping me safe," I said.

We were standing on what would be the sidewalk if anything except snow was visible.

"No problem," he said.

"Did you want to warm up before you head home?" An image of us snuggling in front of the fire popped into my head. I hastily added, "I could make some hot chocolate."

"Thanks, but Nathalie's waiting." He held up the videos.

"Oh, right. I'm glad she's feeling better."

"Yeah."

I expected him to leave. But he just stood there.

"Look, about this afternoon—"

"I don't want to talk about it," I said hastily.

He nodded. "You kissed me back."

"I said I don't want to talk about it."

"I know. I just . . . I'm feeling guilty."

"That's good. I mean, I respect that you feel bad about what happened."

"Yeah, well . . ."

"I do too. She's been so nice to me."

"How do you do it? How do you date a bunch of different guys?"

I was cold. I wanted to go inside. But I wanted to stay out here, too. I wanted to talk with Josh. Shoot. I wanted to kiss him again.

Instead, I shrugged. "I just never went on a date with a guy who made me not want to go out with someone else. If that makes sense."

"It does. Sorta. I mean, I think I get what you're saying. So if I didn't have a girlfriend, how many dates would we have?"

I released a big sigh. "Hard to say."

"What's the most you've ever had with one guy?"

"Three."

"It must be hard to break up with someone."

"There's no breaking up. We just stop dating."

"Right."

"Nathalie's probably wondering where you are."

"Probably. I'd better go." He tapped the DVD clutched in my gloved hand. "Call if you get scared."

He turned on his heel and walked away. I should have gone into the house, but I didn't. I stood there until I couldn't see him anymore.

I hadn't even started to watch the movie yet, and I was scared.

Scared that I'd never meet anyone I wanted to be with as badly as I wanted to be with Josh.

13

The next morning I woke up and could barely move my legs without moaning. Apparently the day before I'd used muscles in my thighs that I hadn't even realized I had.

I hobbled down the stairs. It was really quiet on the second floor. No one was working yet.

I slowly made my way to the kitchen. Mom and Mr. Wynter were sitting at the table drinking coffee. The room smelled like bacon and maple syrup. Mom must have fixed breakfast.

"Are you okay?" Mom asked.

"Yeah, just a little sore from the trek I made yesterday." I shuffled to the counter and poured my coffee, prepped it just the way I liked it, and took a long sip.

Leaning against the counter, I thought about asking if Josh was here. But would that make them wonder why I cared?

"Why don't you come sit down?" Mom asked.

"Because I'm afraid if I sit, I may never be able to get back up." I glanced over at Mr. Wynter. "I guess Josh isn't sore."

"I doubt it, but he had something to take care of today, so he won't be working with me."

I was surprised by the disappointment that hammered into me. I looked out the window at the mounds of white and thought of kissing in the snow . . .

Great, just great. Was everything going to remind me of him?

I spent the morning finishing off the stenciling in the guestroom—although my thighs protested climbing the ladder. Then I went to my bedroom and began designing the website for the B&B. Mom had already given me a lot of the information that she wanted to publicize, so I just had to organize it, design some graphics, and use the creative side of my brain.

I love doing the layout of a new page, and normally, I get lost in the process. But today I found myself staring through the window toward Nathalie's house, wondering if what Josh had to do involved being with her. Maybe he was feeding her chicken noodle soup. Rubbing her feet. Warming up blankets for her.

Confessing that he'd kissed me.

I didn't understand why I kept thinking about him. I never thought about a guy this much.

The knock outside my room barely registered with me.

"Door's open!"

It opened slowly, and Josh peered inside. "Actually, it's not."

I tried to act calm and cool by just sitting in my chair, but it's one of those with a swiveling seat and I almost made myself dizzy by how much half swiveling I was doing, one way, then the other, back and forth, back and forth.

"That's just an expression," I said.

"But it's wrong."

I couldn't believe how glad I was to see him. "Yeah, well, I wasn't expecting Mr. Dictionary."

Grinning, he tossed something at me. I caught the plastic jar before it crashed to the floor. "What's this?"

"A warm therapy gel. You rub it on your legs to help ease the stiffness."

"How did you know I was stiff?"

"Lucky guess."

I wrapped both my hands around it. "Thanks. I am pretty sore."

"The balm is all-natural. I use it all the time after games. I brought you something else, too."

He opened the door wider and carried in a bookshelf.

"Oh, wow!" I set the jar on the desk and got to my feet. Groaning with the sudden movement, I walked toward him like I'd turned into a zombie.

The shelf fit perfectly in the little nook where the ceiling slanted. At the narrow end where books couldn't fit, he'd put little cubbyholes.

"Thought you could put your little mice in those," he said.

"That's great!" I ran my hand over one of the smooth shelves. "I didn't expect it to be this nice. Really, I don't know how to thank you."

I looked at him then and sorta wished I hadn't, because I had a feeling he was thinking that a kiss would be a great way to say thank you.

"How's Nathalie?" I felt compelled to ask, to remind him—and me—that there was someone else.

"She's good."

"I'm glad."

"Yeah, me too."

Our conversation was in danger of putting me to sleep.

He moved from beneath the low ceiling so he could stand up straight.

"I can't stop thinking about you," he said.

Okay, that woke me up.

"You have to." I moved to the desk and picked up the jar. "Thanks for everything."

"Do you think about me?"

"Not really."

"Not at all?"

"Look, there's another woman in my dad's life, and I don't like the way it makes me feel or makes my mom feel, so I'm not going to do that to someone."

He nodded. "You're right. So, you going on the hayride tonight?"

"Is there a reason I shouldn't?"

Or a reason that it's any of your business?

"Nah, I was just curious."

"Yeah, I'm planning to go."

"Good. I'll catch you later, then."

I watched him walk out of my room. Then I looked at the shelves and I knew I'd lied.

Did I think about him?

Almost every minute of every hour since he'd kissed me.

14

I figured the best way to stop thinking about Josh was to focus on Chase. Maybe I'd even break my dating record with him and go for an amazing four dates.

So I decided to take this hayride seriously. I was going to wear knockout clothes. Or as close to knockout as I could get and still be warm. Which actually, when I got right down to it, meant no knockout at all.

I stuffed the legs of my jeans into my fur-lined boots and mentally patted myself on the back for being smart enough to purchase them. My feet, at least, should be warm, especially since I'd insulated them with two layers of socks.

I wore a thin sweater beneath my thick sweater and wrapped a woolen scarf around my neck.

Since the goal was to capture Chase's attention, I decided to go without a woolen cap pulled down over my ears. I mean, how cold could it be?

In the wagon, wouldn't the sides act as a buffer against the wind? And wouldn't I be snuggled against Chase anyway?

I thought about wearing my leather jacket. It was usually all I wore during the winter in Texas. But when I looked outside and saw a few flakes of snow drifting through the glow of the street lamps, I decided to be more practical. I put on my thick parka, which pretty much ruined the hot look I'd been trying to attain.

Unless I wore it unzipped. Then it didn't look too bad. I would have to see how long I could go with the cold wind battering my chest before I gave in and zipped it up.

"Zip up your coat," Mom said when I came downstairs.

"Mom, I'll be fine."

Chase was standing in the entryway. I wondered if Mr. Wynter could wire the doorbell so it would sound in my bedroom. I never knew when people had arrived.

Chase was wearing jeans, a sweater with polar bears on it, and a jacket that wasn't buttoned. I had a feeling he wouldn't button it, no matter how cold the night got.

"I told Shanna to pick us up here," he said. "Hope that's okay."

"Sure."

An uneasy silence filled the space—probably because Mom was standing there. I said something I thought I'd never say. "Why don't we wait outside, so we don't miss her?"

"Sounds great."

Mom told me again to zip up my coat before she instructed us to have fun.

Chase and I stood on the porch. I stuffed my gloved hands into my jacket and hunched my shoulders against the cold. I cursed and zipped up my jacket.

Chase laughed.

"It's not funny," I said. "I'm trying to fit in."

He touched my cheek. How could his bare hand be warm?

"You fit in just fine," he said.

I stomped my feet on the porch. Another attempt at generating warmth.

"You know, you need a swing on this porch," he said.

"Great idea. I'll let Mom know."

Maybe I should dart inside right now and tell her.

I heard sleigh bells chiming and felt a little thrill. Even though there was the potential for disaster—or at the very least, awkwardness—I was really excited and looking forward to the hayride and spending time with Chase.

"There they are," he said, taking my arm and helping me down the steps.

Two wagons on runners, pulled by what looked to be Clydesdales, came to a stop in front of the inn. Lots of hay was visible and I clearly saw everyone sitting there because there was nothing obstructing my view.

"I thought wagons had sides," I said.

"Oh, sure, wagons do," Chase said. "These are technically called drays."

"Oh."

I almost followed that comment with another "oh" when I saw Josh and Nathalie on the dray Chase was walking toward. Corey and Adam, as well as Shanna and Rand, were also there. I recognized the man driving the first team. He was the one who'd delivered our boxes of stuff. I figured he was Shanna's dad.

As we neared, Josh scooted to the side, leaned over, and offered his hand. I thought about asking Chase if the other dray had room, but since he'd already put his hands on my waist to boost me up, I just put my hand in Josh's. He pulled, Chase lifted, and before I knew it, I was rolling in the hay, so to speak.

Josh gave Chase his hand, and Chase vaulted

onto the wagon. He settled down beside me.

I smiled at Nathalie. "I'm glad you're feeling better."

"I wouldn't miss the hayride." She snuggled up against Josh, her back to his chest. He put his arms around her. "My boyfriend will keep me nice and warm."

With a lurch, the wagon started to glide forward. I released a little unexpected squeal as I lost my balance. Chase chuckled, helping me to right myself and managing to maneuver so my back was to his chest and he was supporting me.

"I can't believe you don't do hayrides in Texas," he said.

I held up my hands and twisted around to look at him. "Again, city girl."

"I'm glad you got here in time for the hayride," Shanna said. "It's one of my favorite things to do in the winter."

"Is that your dad driving?" I asked.

"Yeah."

"He delivered our stuff," I said, just to have something to say.

Shanna laughed. "He does a lot of that." She pointed behind us. "That's my brother, Tom, driving that wagon."

Then she snuggled against Rand, and I figured

that meant an end to the conversation.

I glanced back over at Nathalie. Her eyes were closed and her head was nestled against Josh's shoulder. I tried not to think about how nice that might feel.

I shifted my gaze a little and it clashed with Josh's. He was watching me, a little too intently.

I turned my attention to the night sky. I became very much aware of the straw poking into my backside. Romance at its finest? Hardly.

I had a feeling this was going to be the longest night of my life.

We left the lights of town behind and turned onto a path that I guess was a normal paved road in the summer. It rose up slightly and wound around. Tonight the path was lit by a full moon, and I was amazed by how much light it provided. Back home, the city lights washed moonlight out, but here, it was actually pretty amazing.

I don't know how long we traveled before we turned onto another path. My backside was numb from the cold and I wasn't feeling the straw anymore. Sometime during the ride, Chase had stuck his hands in my jacket pockets—the macho guy way of keeping hands warm, I guess.

Up ahead, I spotted the welcoming lights of a house.

"That's Shanna's house," Josh said to me, maybe realizing that I had no idea where we were.

"You kids ready to go in and warm up for a while?" Shanna's dad called back to us.

I didn't know if it would be cool to yell "Yes!" so I kept quiet. But everyone else responded with various affirmatives, none nearly as enthusiastic as mine would have been.

When the wagon came to a stop, Chase pushed me forward a little bit, needing room so he could get off the wagon.

Turning, I watched as he helped Nathalie down.

Huh? Wasn't that interesting?

Josh jumped off the wagon and reached for me.

"I've got her," Chase said, shoving Josh to the side.

"Okay," Josh said, but he was looking at me as he said it. Then he turned, took Nathalie's hand, and headed toward the house.

"Hope you're okay with me helping Nathalie first," Chase said, once he helped me down. "She was ready."

"No problem. It's taking me a while to thaw out and move."

Chase took my hand. "We'll get you some cider. You'll be warm in no time."

Although we were the last ones inside, plenty of cider was still available. I wasn't sure if it was really apple cider, because it tasted like mint. Really yummy. I nibbled on a warm brownie, fresh from the oven. No wonder Shanna's family had this routine down to an art; they did it every year.

I turned to say something to Chase. He was looking toward the corner of the kitchen where Nathalie and Josh were talking. He must have felt my gaze on him, because he turned his attention to me, and his cheeks were red. Was he embarrassed that I caught him looking at her?

"I'm going to get some more cider. You want some?" he asked.

"No, I'm good."

"The den is through there," he said, pointing toward a hallway. "They have a huge fireplace if you want to get warm."

"And if I don't want to get warm, they don't have a huge fireplace?"

He grinned. "Either way they have a huge fireplace. Everyone warms up in there before we hop back on the hay. Why don't you go save us a spot?"

"Okay."

I found the den with no problem. Corey and

Adam were sitting together on an ottoman. Not only was the fireplace huge but so was the room. I wandered along the back wall, which was mostly covered with shelves, and looked at all the carousel horse figurines displayed.

"Shanna's mom has a thing for carousels," Josh said quietly beside me.

I hadn't heard him come into the room. I glanced over at him. "I can't blame her. There's something appealing about them."

"Are you having fun?"

"Oh, yeah. I especially like the moments when I'm warm."

"I'd keep you warm if I could."

"I think you have someone else to keep warm," I reminded him. "I'm glad she was able to make it."

"Yeah, me too. I would have hated missing the hay ride."

"So you would have missed it if she couldn't come?"

He studied me for a long moment. "Yeah. It would have been . . . best, probably. Not to come if she couldn't."

"You're a good boyfriend."

He shrugged. "So how do you like Chase?"

"He's nice. A lot of fun." *And I think he might*

like your girlfriend.

"How are your legs?"

I gave him an odd look. "Long? Warm?"

"Sore?"

I laughed lightly. "Sorry. I didn't know what you were asking, but yes, no, they're feeling a lot better. The salve helped. Although I'll probably be stiff again in the morning."

"Probably." He creased his brow. "Did you bring a cap?"

I shook my head. "I didn't figure islanders would be wearing them."

"You thought wrong." He held out a black knitted hat. "You'll want this later."

I started to reach for it. Then stopped. "I really shouldn't."

"It doesn't mean anything. I'm just more used to the cold than you are."

"What about Nathalie?"

"She brought something."

And she has you.

I took the cap and stuffed it into my coat pocket, looking around, making sure no one noticed, like we were exchanging something illegal. "Thanks."

"Well." He took a step back. "I'm glad you came on the hayride."

"Me too."

He turned just as Nathalie came into the room, Chase right behind her. Maybe I should have felt jealous. But I didn't. I didn't even wonder what they were doing together.

But when Nathalie snuggled up against Josh, that's when I began to wish I hadn't come.

We stopped at two more houses. Everyone had their own apple cider recipe and favorite snack to offer. Josh seemed to make a point of avoiding me. I was glad. I'd never had what my dad called a poker face, and I worried that my expression would reveal how much I liked him, which wasn't fair to Nathalie or Chase . . . or Josh.

It was a little strange how many times I discovered Chase looking at Nathalie. He always gave me an embarrassed grin and asked some question about Texas. It seemed to be the only thing we had to discuss.

After we visited the last house—and I knew it was the last house because we started traveling back the way we'd come—everyone was snuggled deeper in the straw. I'd pulled Josh's cap down over my head and ears long before we headed home. I wasn't an islander yet, and I got tired of pretending. Okay, I got too cold to pretend.

Corey and Adam were doing some serious kissing. Josh was just holding Nathalie. Probably didn't want to catch her cold or flu or whatever it was she had. It looked like she'd gone to sleep against his shoulder again. Every now and then, Shanna and Rand would sneak a kiss.

"She worries that her dad will look back here," Chase whispered, holding me more tightly.

"I don't blame her. That would be really weird."

"Yeah."

I thought maybe he'd kiss me. But he didn't even try.

Since we'd been the last ones picked up, we were the first ones dropped off. Chase and I stood on the walkway, watching the dray move on up the street.

"Well, that was fun," I said.

"Nathalie probably shouldn't have come out tonight."

"Do you worry about her?"

He looked surprised. "No, just an observation."

"You've known her a long time."

"I've known everyone on the island a long time."

"I guess I mean, you know her really well."

"Ditto, on knowing everyone really well."

"But you work together."

"Are you going somewhere with this?"

He sounded seriously ticked off.

"Ah, no, just making an observation."

"It's just . . ."

"She's had a boyfriend forever," I said.

"Yeah. I mean, when I was twelve I wasn't thinking about girls really. She's never had a chance to see if she might like someone better."

"Someone like you?"

He sighed. "I guess I'm not as good at hiding it as I used to be."

"You know, flirting with other girls in the fudge shop might not be the way to go if you're trying to get her attention."

"It's the only time she notices me. I thought if she thought lots of girls liked me, maybe she would too." He rubbed his hands up and down his face. "So now that you know my deep dark secret, do you still want to go to V.P. with me tomorrow night?"

Considering I had a deep, dark secret of my own?

"Yeah, sure."

"Great. I'll see you then." He turned and headed up the street.

I didn't know whether to be disappointed or

relieved. I suppose if nothing else we could commiserate together.

I opened the gate and walked up the porch to the house. Light was shining out from the parlor window. I should have known Mom would still be up. What sort of report should I give her?

I'd barely closed the front door before she popped out of the parlor. "We have our first guests!"

Not now. I wanted to be excited, I wanted to be welcoming. I really, really did. I wanted to be the perfect hostess, but I *needed* to crawl into bed and go to sleep so I could stop thinking about Josh.

"Come on in and meet them," Mom said.

"Oh, Mom, I'm really wiped out—"

"No excuses. This is a unique opportunity to learn to be a good hostess."

She was so excited that I just couldn't disappoint her. Forcing myself to smile, I went into the parlor.

Our guest flung her arms wide. "Surprise!"

"Tara!"

I rushed toward her, she ran toward me. Then we were hugging and laughing, both of us talking at once. It was so good to see her. Nothing had changed. Her hair was still black, her eyes still blue. Her nose was still slightly crooked. When she was six, her brother tried to teach her how to play baseball. He told her to keep her eye on the ball. She did—until it hit her in the nose.

"Are you surprised? You look surprised."

"Why didn't you tell me you were coming?" I asked.

"If I had, it wouldn't have been a surprise."

"When did you decide—"

"A couple of nights ago. But we couldn't get a direct flight, and we've been traveling all day and night. I didn't think we'd ever get here!"

"We?"

We finally broke apart, and I could see past her into the room. Shaun lifted his hand in greeting. "Hey."

"Hi."

I didn't know him well enough to rush forward and hug him—for which he was no doubt grateful. Still, I said the honest-to-gosh truth. "I'm so glad y'all are here."

"Josh kissed you?" Tara asked.

We were in my bed, snuggled beneath the quilts. We'd visited downstairs for a couple of hours, before we decided to call it a night. Mom gave Shaun a room on the second floor. She'd readied another room for Tara, but we'd had too many sleepovers together to sleep in separate rooms now.

Once we turned out the lights, I'd filled her in on the past two days of my life.

"What a player," she said with obvious disgust.

"He seemed as surprised as I was. I mean, I don't think he really meant to kiss me. It just happened."

"So what are you going to do?" she asked.

"Pretend it didn't happen."

"What about this other guy, this Chase?"

"I like him."

"But not as much."

"That could just be because I don't know him as well. Besides, he has a thing for Nathalie too."

"She must be something else. I can't wait to meet her."

Even though it was dark, I grinned so broadly that I thought my jaw would ache in the morning. "I can't believe you're here."

"What are best friends for?"

"How long can you stay?"

"Only until Monday, just long enough to get my Ash fix. I swear, I don't know what I'd do if I didn't have Shaun."

"I can't believe he came with you."

"He's my rock."

"I wish you'd gotten here early enough to go on the hayride."

"I can't believe Chase didn't kiss you. I mean, a hayride sounds like a kissing thing."

"I was a little surprised too, but if he had, I think it would have been only to get Nathalie's attention. So I really like him for not using me like that."

"I guess. So, tomorrow, I've got big plans for us," Tara said.

"What?"

"A fudge run."

"That's the reason you're really here, isn't it?" I teased. "You came for the fudge, not me."

"You know it. And I brought disguises so we can check out all the fudge shops, not just Nathalie's."

I laughed. It just felt so right having Tara here.

She threw one of my stuffed animals at me. "Night, Ash."

The bed wobbled as she rolled onto her side. I looked out the window. The next few days were going to be so much fun. Tara was always fun.

Then, because it was dark, and she'd started to snore, I slipped out of bed and went to where I'd dropped my jacket earlier. I reached into the pocket and pulled out Josh's cap. I worked it down over my head, over my ears. I crawled into bed and fell asleep doing what I knew I shouldn't: dreaming about him.

15

The next morning when I woke up, Tara wasn't in my room. I wasn't surprised. She's a morning person.

I got dressed and went downstairs. Just as I suspected, Tara was in the kitchen helping Mom make breakfast. Mr. Wynter, Josh, and Shaun were sitting at the oak table, finishing off a batch of pancakes.

"Hey, sleepyhead," Mom said brightly when I walked into the kitchen.

I grunted. Tara handed me my coffee mug. I filled it quickly, added my milk and sugar, and took my first sip.

"Watching Ash drink coffee is kinda like watching a werewolf movie," Tara said. "You can see the transformation from man into beast."

"Except for me, it's beast into girl, I know," I said sourly and took another sip.

"Want some pancakes?" Mom asked.

"No, thanks." I leaned against the counter.

"They're really good," Josh said. He was watching me like he was hoping to see the transformation that Tara was talking about.

"Tara is really into cooking," I told him. I held up a hand. "Don't say it. I know I'm not into cooking, breakfast, or early morning, but here I am."

Once Shaun finished off another batch of pancakes, he, Tara, and I headed toward the downtown shops.

"Okay, Josh is hot," Tara said as we were walking.

"Tell me something I don't already know," I said.

"He likes you."

"He has a girlfriend," I reminded her.

"Will we meet her?"

"If she's working today. She may have relapsed after being in the cold last night."

She wasn't working, but Chase was. Tara thought he was hot too. Not that she said it out loud, but I could tell by the way her eyes lit up when he offered her free fudge.

While she and Shaun were looking over the selections, Chase urged me closer and said, "So what about tonight?"

"Tonight?"

"Our date."

"Oh, right." I hit the side of my head, like I was trying to knock some sense into myself. I was hoping he'd laugh, but he didn't.

"I didn't forget. Well, okay, I did. I didn't know Tara was coming."

"We can do it another time, or they can join us."

"A double date?"

"Sure. We don't have many of those here."

I smiled. "Are you sure you wouldn't mind? They're only going to be here a few days, so I do want to spend as much time with them as I can. And I don't want to not go out with you."

He smiled at that. "It's not a problem. I'll come by at seven. It'll be fun."

We left the shop right after Tara made her choices.

"Okay, I know this might not be fair, but I want to buy fudge from every shop that's open so I can do a taste comparison," Tara said.

"Fudge is fudge," Shaun said.

"A lot you know," she said, handing him the bag. "You get to carry it all for me."

We did a taste test at every shop and always made a purchase afterward. Other than the shopping I'd done earlier in the week with Nathalie and her friends, I hadn't visited many of the other stores. Tara is a shop-till-she-drops kind of girl.

A lot of the stores weren't open so she considered it a real find whenever we ran across one that was.

We walked up the hill to see the huge, white hotel where some old movie had been made.

"It's like something straight out of the novels my mom reads. I can picture women in long dresses with parasols walking through the gardens here in the summer," Tara said. "And you said actors hang out around here, right?"

"Apparently Nathalie had a sighting, but winter is probably not the best time to do a movie-star hunt," I said.

"I guess not."

We walked back toward Chateau Ashleigh, then went past it to the island lighthouse, where we were able to take a tour.

When we finally got home, Tara insisted on going into the backyard and building a snowman.

I thought about taking her to see the bat cave, but I wasn't certain I could find it. And asking Josh to go with us probably wasn't a smart move.

Especially when I kept thinking about how much fun it would have been to have shared the day with him, too.

* * *

In the summer, I figured V.P. would be packed, but that night when Shaun, Tara, Chase, and I arrived, maybe a dozen kids were hanging around.

I wasn't surprised to see Nathalie, but I was taken aback when she made a place at our table for her and Josh—mostly because I was still worried that she'd realize her boyfriend had kissed me. And that I'd kissed him back.

"You don't mind, do you?" she asked.

"No, of course not," I said. "Friends make room for friends."

"And we're best friends!" she said.

Sometimes she was a little over the top, but it was part of her charm. I couldn't not like her, and I so didn't want to hurt her.

"Tomorrow night is the Victorian Walk," she said to Tara and Shaun. "I'm selling tickets. All proceeds benefit the Historical Preservation Society. You get to walk through the old Victorian houses and the night ends with a dance at *the* Hotel."

While the island had other hotels, I'd already learned that there was only one "*the* Hotel"—the large one on the hill that had been used as a setting for a movie.

"And best all"—she paused for emphasis—"everyone goes in costume."

"What? Like Halloween?" Shaun asked.

Nathalie looked at him as if he had spoken in a language she didn't understand. "No. We all wear Victorian dresses."

"I'm not wearing a dress," Shaun said.

Nathalie rolled her eyes. "The girls wear dresses. The guys wear suits. It's totally fun. My boyfriend and I already have our costumes, but tomorrow I can meet you at the shop that rents the Victorian clothes. We'll have a blast picking out the perfect outfits for you."

Okay, I had to admit that in the past few days I'd started to develop an appreciation for the houses on the island. And what better way to get to know our neighbors than to take a walk through their houses? On one hand, it seemed a little nosy, but on the other hand, I figured I could learn a lot about fitting in.

I looked at Tara and smiled. "I think it could be fun."

"I'm in. It'll sure be something we've never done before."

"Great," Nathalie said. "I'll bring the tickets over tomorrow. They're twenty dollars each."

"Dude, no way," Shaun said.

"It all goes to an important cause," Nathalie emphasized. "All my best friends go."

And as we all knew, I was one of her best friends.

"I'll take care of the tickets," I said. "Mom and Dad always support charity events. One of them will spring for it. No problem."

"Excellent," Nathalie said. "You won't regret it. It's totally awesome."

While she went on to explain some of the things we could expect tomorrow night, I snuck a glance at Josh. It was obvious that he was trying really hard not to look at me, not to show any interest.

The bad thing was, it made me like him even more.

"So listen, my boyfriend and I have to go sell some more tickets. I'll catch up with you tomorrow at Forever in Time," Nathalie finally said.

"Isn't that a photo studio?" I asked. I remembered passing it on one of my walks.

"Yeah, it's one of those places where people dress in clothes from another era and have their photos taken. They have lots of costumes, so they rent them out for the Victorian Walk. It's not like we have an abundance of tourists at the moment. So are we a go?"

"Definitely a go," I told her. I knew it would be fun, especially since I wasn't wearing ink on my forehead saying "I kissed your boyfriend," so she'd never know.

I watched Josh take Nathalie's hand as they walked away.

I forced myself to turn my attention to Chase. "I'm starving."

"Josh said he took you to the bat cave," Chase said.

I nodded. "Did he tell you we woke up the bats?"

"Said it was the most memorable trip he'd ever taken to the cave."

I had a feeling he wasn't referring only to what happened with the bats.

The waitress came over and took our order. After we finished eating, Chase and Shaun went to play darts. I really liked Chase, and he was fun, but we both knew he was with me only because he couldn't be with Nathalie. And I was with him because . . . well, I didn't even want to think about that.

Weren't we a great pair?

Tara leaned toward me. "I didn't want to say anything in front of Chase, but does Nathalie even know Josh's name?"

"You caught on to the 'my boyfriend' thing, huh?"

"Totally. It's like okay, I got it, you've got a boyfriend."

"It's sorta like he's a trophy."

"No kidding."

"Although to be honest, I don't think I've ever heard her call anyone by name. I'm her new best friend, by the way."

Tara laughed. "Yeah, well, you're my old best friend and you know what they say about old friends."

"They're gold."

She touched her mug of hot chocolate against mine. "You better believe it, girlfriend."

The next morning Shaun opted out of going to the photography studio/costume shop. He wanted to hang with Josh—which meant inhaling paint fumes all day, but whatever. And I was grateful to have some time with Tara. We'd stayed up really late again talking in bed, but we still had so much to talk about.

"Shaun just bailed because he knows I want some girl time with you," Tara said as we walked toward the business end of town. "He's great that way."

"You're really crazy about him," I said.

"Oh, yeah. I know he's pretty much stuck in one emotion level, but it works for us."

"That's all that matters," I said, and I really meant it.

"So what we have to do now is find you a boyfriend," she announced.

"You know how I feel about having a boyfriend."

"I know, but come on. There aren't many guys here, and if you don't lock on to one of them, you're gonna have a lot of dateless nights."

"I'm not worried. I think Chase will always be available for a date or just to hang out."

"How many dateable guys are on this island, anyway?"

"I don't know."

"The way Nathalie was hawking the tickets for tonight's thing—"

"Victorian Walk."

"—well, we're bound to see a lot of guys for you to look over. And Shaun is a great judge of character."

Yeah, that was what I wanted: for Shaun of the Dead to select my boyfriend for me.

Thirty minutes later, Tara and I were standing in the back room of the photography studio, staring in a mirror at our Victorian getups. Her dress was a deep blue, mine a lilac. They had bustles and trains, flounces and lace. We were wearing gloves that wouldn't keep our hands warm on a cool day.

"I feel like one of the heroines in those books my mom reads," Tara said.

"And *you* read," I reminded her.

"Well, yeah," Tara said.

"Hats, hats, hats," Nathalie said, breaking into our discussion, "you've got to have hats."

She'd been waiting at the shop, like a toddler anxious to unwrap a present.

"I just love period costumes," she said now, lifting from the shelf a wide-brimmed hat with a dark purple satin bow on the crown. She set it on my head, angled it one way, then the other. "There. What do you think?"

It was a little big and I had to lift it to really see. Tara snorted. I giggled. "I don't know. I'm not really a hat person."

Unless it was a Texas Rangers baseball cap.

"Who is, these days?" Nathalie asked. "But this is the Victorian era. Women wouldn't be caught dead going out without a hat. Guys, either."

I turned and looked at her. "You mean the guys are going to be wearing hats?"

"Oh, yeah. They'll be wearing top hats, bowlers. People really go all out for this event. Well, actually, we go all out for everything. It's what makes living on the island so much fun. Our enthusiasm."

"I can't see Shaun wearing a hat unless it's a knit cap pulled down over his ears," Tara said.

"My boyfriend can convince him, trust me," Nathalie said.

I expected Tara to give me a secret smile. Instead, she said, "You do realize your boyfriend has a name, right?"

"Well, duh? Yes! What kind of question is that?"

"Just checking."

"We need to find you a hat," Nathalie said and went back over to the wall to find one.

I adjusted the one I was wearing. "I don't know. How crowded will it be tonight? I'm afraid I'll run into people if I'm wearing this."

"It is kinda wide," Tara admitted.

"I guess it's okay for walking outdoors, but walking through a house or in a ballroom . . . I just don't know."

Nathalie came back over and tugged my hat back into place. "It'll be fine. Trust me on this."

She perched a much smaller hat on Tara's head and declared, "Perfect!"

It was actually more of a bonnet. Narrow, with feathers circling the crown and brim.

"Maybe something smaller like that would be

better for me," I said.

"Smaller won't go with your dress," Nathalie said.

"Are there going to be costume police at this thing?" I asked.

Nathalie laughed lightly. "Of course not, but you don't want people thinking you don't know the first thing about accessorizing. After all, the society section of the newspaper will have a write-up describing who wore what."

"Who would care?" Tara asked.

"It's just the way it was done back then. We really get into the time period," Nathalie explained.

"Okay, then, I think I can make this work," I said, tilting the hat back up.

Nathalie tapped it back down.

"It really cuts down on my visibility," I said.

"You'll get used to it," Nathalie assured me. "Let's find you some button-up shoes."

She not only found us shoes that didn't pinch our toes too badly, but she also found us velvet, fur-lined capes.

The photographer took photos of Tara and me before we removed our costumes. He promised the pictures would be ready before the end of the day so Tara could take her copy back to Texas with her.

I was having way too much fun with Tara here. I didn't want to think about her leaving. And I was afraid it was going to be difficult, lonely even, when she went home.

16

In the end, Nathalie's boyfriend didn't talk Shaun into wearing a top hat or a bowler. He wore exactly what Tara had predicted: a knit cap pulled down over his ears. He wore jeans, boots, a sweatshirt, and a heavy down jacket. Not exactly Victorian attire, but Tara was convinced Nathalie had exaggerated about everyone's enthusiasm for wearing costumes.

"I suspect it's only the women who really dress up," she said.

Although I wasn't sure if people were even going to be able to tell that we were dressed up. I loved the fur-lined cape, but it was a lot colder at night than during the day. Tara and I had just got to the end of the walkway—hadn't even gone through the gate yet—when we turned around and went back inside to get our heavy coats.

Yes, that meant we were clearly identifiable as

nonislanders, but we both decided that was better than being human ice pops.

Of course, Shaun didn't care what Tara wore. She could have been in Eskimo attire and he would have been fine with it.

Mom was going on the tour as well, with some women she'd met when she joined The Ladies' Tea Group. Apparently they liked to get together once a week to sample assorted teas and exchange sandwich recipes. I had to admit that it had been a long time since I'd seen Mom this relaxed and happy. Moving was definitely paying off.

Tara, Shaun, and I walked through the shopping area of town. Most of the houses designated for the Victorian Walk were along a curving hill that would eventually lead back to the hotel where the dance was being held—at least, that was how it appeared on the map we'd been given at the base of the hill. The path was clearly marked with strings of white Christmas lights. The houses we were allowed to enter had a sign in front of them announcing:

Victorian Walk Tour
Donations Accepted at the Door
All Proceeds to Benefit the Historical Preservation Society

Nathalie had forgotten to mention that the tickets were for getting into the dance only. To take a tour through one of the cottages, we were encouraged to make a donation at the door. Since Tara and I didn't have purses to match our costumes—we certainly didn't want an unfavorable review in the society section—we didn't have any money on us, so it fell to Shaun to dig out his wallet and drop a donation into the bowl for us. He didn't seem to mind, but then with him it was hard to tell.

The first cottage was totally awesome. Nearly every room had a fireplace and they all had a fire going. The rooms were huge, which was good because a lot of people were walking through and I was wearing that stupid hat. Not only was my visibility limited, but I was much wider than normal. After bumping into a couple of people, I took off the hat and just hoped I wouldn't run into Nathalie.

When we went through the kitchen, we were given a plastic cup of hot apple cider and a brownie. That seemed to be the standard policy for each house: some sort of hot apple cider (cinnamon, raspberry, red hots) and a dessert (cookie, lemon bar, cupcake, brownie). Some rooms had a rope in the doorway so you could only peer inside, but most allowed you to walk through.

I've never been big into touring homes. Mom and Dad used to go to a Parade of Homes, but those were new houses built for the megawealthy, valued at millions. Dream homes for most people. I'd gone once but hadn't been really interested after that.

But I had to admit that touring these older homes was more interesting. I tried to imagine all the different people who had lived here during the past hundred or so years. They may have even owned some of the knickknacks sitting on the shelves.

And we discovered that Nathalie hadn't exaggerated. Most people were dressed in period costumes—even the men. Top hats and walking canes and everything.

After we toured the fourth house and were walking along the path, Shaun said, "I've got enough money for one more house."

Tara wrapped her arm around his and snuggled up against him. "That's cool. I've pretty much seen all I need to see. Seen one house, seen them all."

I wasn't sure if she was trying to make Shaun feel better because he hadn't brought more money, or if she really hadn't liked walking through the houses.

"I thought they were cool," I admitted, feeling kinda geeky because I'd enjoyed looking around a lot more than I'd expected. I was already looking forward to next year. And who knew? Maybe Mom and I would put our place on the tour. "Thanks, Shaun, for making the donations, so we could walk through them."

"You really thought they were interesting?" Tara asked.

"Well, yeah." Maybe I'd been browsing through too many of Mom's Victorian books. I knew the architecture, the furniture. Maybe an appreciation of this stuff just came from living on the island.

"Then you pick the last house we go through," Shaun said.

I shook my head. "I don't want you to spend all your money on the tour. I'll pay you back when we get home."

"Don't worry about it. I've kept some money in reserve."

"Shaun is great with money," Tara said. "He budgets an exact amount for different things and he sticks to it. Me, I spend until it's all gone. That's my budget plan."

"Which isn't really a budget or a plan," Shaun said.

I wondered if Shaun would end up being an accountant.

"Okay, so pick a house," Tara said, clearly not wanting to get into her spending habits.

"We'll stop if I see something that looks really amazing," I said.

We rounded the curve in the road, and I spotted it. A huge cottage with a wraparound porch. Turrets were situated on either side. I wanted to walk through it; I really did. I didn't want Shaun spending more money on us, but if I didn't take a tour now, it would be another year before I'd have a chance.

"Uh-oh," Tara said. "Ash is salivating."

"I am not," I protested. "Okay, I am. I haven't walked to this side of the island yet. I didn't know this was here."

"It is pretty awesome looking," Shaun said.

"It reminds me of one of those places in those horror movies you watch—only this one isn't falling down," Tara said. "So you want to go take a peek?"

"A peek costs as much as a tour," I said.

"Okay, so let's do the tour. Then we'll head to the hotel for some real fun," Tara said.

People were strolling down the walkway as we strode up. It was silly for me to be this excited about touring the house. We stepped through the open doorway—

"Oh, you finally made it," Nathalie said. Before I could respond, she added, "This is my boyfriend's house. Isn't it amazing? I'm serving as hostess. I do every year. And you're not wearing your hat."

She snatched it out of my hands and plopped it on my head. I expected her to flash her costume police badge.

"And what is with the coat?" she asked.

"It's like negative a thousand degrees out there," I explained.

"People are going to mistake you for a fudgie," Nathalie said.

"What's wrong with that?" Tara asked. "We both love fudge."

Tara had obviously forgotten what I'd told her about fudgies. Or maybe she just liked to tease Nathalie.

Nathalie rolled her eyes, obviously too disgusted with both of us to explain. She pointed to her left. "The kitchen is that way. Go warm up with some cider so you can take off your coats."

Edging past her, I walked to the dining room and waited for Tara and Shaun to catch up.

"Okay, her not calling her boyfriend by name was funny last night, but it's really starting to get on my nerves," Tara said when she caught up to me.

"I don't think she calls anyone by name." Guilt over kissing said boyfriend was making me feel a need to defend Nathalie.

"But it's one of those things that if it's true, you don't have to keep shoving it in people's faces," Tara said.

"I don't think she realizes she's shoving anything." I glanced around. "Isn't this place great?"

"Yeah, great," Tara said with as much enthusiasm as Shaun might exhibit. "Let's go get some cider, boyfriend."

Shaun laughed, a deep chortle. I was not only surprised by the sound, but surprised that he'd caught on to Tara's dig at Nathalie.

"Welcome," Mr. Wynter said as we walked into the kitchen. He was holding a delicate china plate adorned with fudge—no doubt from Sweet Temptations. The plate, though, looked odd in his large, beefy hands. "Help yourself to some fudge. Cider's over there."

Josh was over there too, standing beside an island. With a ladle, he was dipping cider out of a crock pot and pouring it into the typical plastic cups.

"Hey," he said, handing each of us a cup.

"Hey," I said back while Tara and Shaun simply nodded. "I can't believe you and your dad live in such a . . . well, I mean, it's not a typical bachelor pad."

"Most of it's my grandma's doing. And my great-grandma's. Dad inherited the place after my grandparents passed. We're third-generation islanders. Keeping the place up is what got Dad into carpentry."

"From what I've seen so far, it's awesome."

"Want a personal tour?"

His question seemed perfectly legit. One friend showing another friend his house.

"Sure." I looked at Tara and Shaun. "Is that okay with y'all?"

"Actually, my toes are killing me. Shaun and I are going to sit over here and rest for a bit. You go ahead."

I hadn't expected to be walking through the house alone with Josh, but several people were wandering around, so it wasn't like we'd be really alone. And it wasn't like he'd do anything—like try to kiss me again—with Nathalie standing in the doorway greeting people.

I looked at Josh and grinned the widest grin ever. "Sure, I'd love a personal tour."

"Great. Let me get Dad to keep an eye on the cider."

He walked over to his dad, said something quietly. I figured he didn't want to start giving everyone personal tours so he was keeping things hush-hush. Then he came back over to me and smiled. "Let's go."

We went through the back of the kitchen into a sunroom.

"Like the hat," he said.

"Oh, shoot, I forgot all about it." I snatched it off. "It's not really me, but Nathalie insisted. You know how she can be."

"Yeah, I do."

"I don't suppose there's someplace around here where I can lose it until Monday when I have to return it."

"Sure there is." He took it and tossed it onto a nearby chair. "Perfect for the décor."

I chuckled. "I don't know about that."

But I wasn't in any hurry to retrieve it.

He showed me into the library. Floor-to-ceiling bookshelves lined the walls. I'd never seen so many books in my life, except at a public or school library.

"Wow, does anyone read this much?" I asked.

"My grandparents did."

On one of the shelves was a pewter-framed black-and-white photograph. "Is this them?" The guy sorta looked like Josh.

"Yeah," Josh said. "Shortly after they got married."

"I don't know if I've ever known anyone who grew up in the house his grandparents lived in. I mean, my parents don't even live in the same city as my grandparents."

"Makes you appreciate family history, I guess. Or at least it did for me."

He showed me the other rooms. On the second floor were the bedrooms. The door to one of the rooms was closed—and locked.

"Didn't want to clean it," he said.

"You've seen my bedroom," I teased.

"You want to see mine?" he asked, his eyes darkening.

I wondered if we were slipping into that dangerous flirting territory again.

I felt my face warm. As a matter of fact, I got so hot that I was close to shedding my coat. "Uh, no, actually that's okay. I've taken enough of your time and Tara is waiting—"

"I want to show you one more thing, something not on the tour." He pointed to a stairway with a rope across it, indicating no trespassing.

"An attic filled with bats?"

He gave me one of those we-have-a-private-joke grins. Then he looked past me to the far stairs where we could hear people.

"Come on." He grabbed my hand. "We need to hurry before people get up here and I have to show everyone."

He slipped beneath the rope, tugging me after him. I wasn't nearly as limber in my parka and Victorian dress.

It wasn't obvious from the hallway, but it was a spiral staircase. I'd always had a thing for spiral staircases. Maybe because in fairy tales it always seemed like the heroine had a room or a prison or bedchamber at the top of a spiral staircase. Plus, it was always a mystery. As you rounded each turn, you never knew what you were going to see.

The staircase opened up into a circular room. One of the turrets. It had windows all around it with the curtains pulled back. Moonlight and streetlights filtered in.

I could make out the shadows of furniture: a couch, some chairs.

"It was my grandmother's reading room," Josh said. "When I was a kid, though, she'd let me play up here. I'd pretend it was my castle."

Taking my hand, he led me over to the window. I could see the lighted bridge. Even at night this room had a spectacular view.

"Oh, wow." I didn't have any words to do it justice.

"During the summer, it's really awesome. I can't tell you how many nights I've stood up here and thought about leaving this island for good."

I shifted my gaze over to him. "Getting off this rock?"

Okay, I was showing off. Knowing the lingo, I felt like a true islander.

"Yeah. Strange thing is, I haven't been thinking about it so much lately."

His voice had gotten really low, really serious, and I had a feeling that I knew where he was going with this, and it was someplace I didn't want to go.

"Thanks for sharing this room with me," I said quickly. "Now whenever I walk by, I'll know exactly what's up here, but gosh, look at the time." I looked at the imaginary watch on my wrist, which I wouldn't have been able to see in the shadows even if it had been real. "Tara's probably going crazy wondering where I am."

"All I've been thinking about is you," he said, as though I hadn't spoken, hadn't interrupted him.

"Don't you get it?" I backed away quickly. "A

new girl moves to town and suddenly you're thinking greener pastures."

"It's not like that."

"Sure, it is. You were perfectly happy with Nathalie before I moved here."

"Was I?"

"Well, you've been together since you were twelve, so yeah. I mean, it's just . . ."

I didn't know what it was.

"I've gotta go."

I hurried down the steps, nearly tripping twice over the long skirt. I was suddenly hating the Victorians. Jeans were so much better for a hasty getaway.

I slipped under the rope. A couple of people in the hallway stopped and stared at me.

"I was looking for the bathroom." I jerked my thumb toward the stairs. "It's not up there. There's nothing up there. It was totally boring."

I hurried past them, figuring I was going to become known as that crazy girl from Texas.

I found Tara and Shaun in the kitchen, exactly as I'd left them.

"Okay, I'm ready to go." I smiled at Mr. Wynter. "You have a beautiful house. I can see why Mom hired you. Thanks."

He looked confused, like maybe he didn't

know what I was thanking him for. I didn't know either, but it just seemed like the thing to say.

Of course the worst part was leaving through the front door. Nathalie smiled brightly. "What did you think? Doesn't my boyfriend have the coolest house?"

"Absolutely."

"Where's your hat?"

"Lost it. See you later."

"Okay. We'll be heading over to the hotel soon. You can dance with my boyfriend if you want."

I so didn't want.

17

"*What was going on back* there?" Tara asked when I finally slowed down.

"Oh, nothing. I was just tired of touring Victorian houses. Like you said, seen one, seen 'em all."

Tara grabbed my arm and spun me around. "Ash, this is me. *What* is going on?"

I took a deep breath. "He says he can't stop thinking about me."

"I could have told you that," Tara said. "It was pretty obvious when we walked in that he was glad to see you."

I pressed my hands to the sides of my head. "What if Nathalie figures it out? I should probably move back home."

That thought caused an unexpected ache in my chest. I was growing fond of the island. But I'd be the island slut if anyone found out what had happened between Josh and me.

"You're not going to move back home," Tara said.

I glowered at her. "You can order the fudge online."

"You're not going to move back home," she repeated.

I nodded. She was right. I wasn't going to leave Mom. I wasn't going to leave the island. "He's thinking about me because I'm a novelty, that's all."

"I don't think that's the reason," Shaun said.

I glared at him. "Trust me, Shaun, a lot is going on here that you don't know about."

"Tara told me he kissed you."

I frowned at Tara. "You told him?"

"Well, yeah, I tell Shaun everything. He's my boyfriend."

"I'm starting to hate that term. 'My boyfriend.'"

"Well, he is. But he's not going to tell anyone." She turned to Shaun. "So since you know more than Ash thinks you do, what do you think is the reason he's thinking about her?"

"Wait," I ordered.

Some people walked past. We all exchanged hellos. When they were far enough away that they couldn't hear us, I said, "Okay. Spill it."

"Uh, actually I can't. I mean, it's a guy code."

"A. Guy. Code?" I asked.

"Yeah, you know, two guys talking guy stuff. Our unwritten code is that we don't talk to babes about it."

"How about your girlfriend? If she tells you stuff, shouldn't you tell her stuff?"

He looked guiltily at Tara. He did have emotions. I felt a little mean about putting him on the spot.

"Never mind," I said. "So what if he's thinking about me? He's not going to break up with Nathalie just to go on a date with me."

"*A* date?" Tara repeated. "You wouldn't make an exception to your no-boyfriend rule for him?"

"A rule doesn't allow for exceptions."

"I so don't get you sometimes."

I almost looked between her and Shaun and said, "Ditto." But no way did I want to hurt either of their feelings. It wasn't worth it to make my point.

"Come on. Let's just go to the dance."

I was numb, physically and emotionally, by the time we reached the hotel. It was a huge place. A front porch ran the length of it. Horse-drawn sleighs were lined up one after another. I guess to provide transport home afterward.

Tara, of course, sighed and snuggled in closer

to Shaun. "I want to go for a ride in one of those."

A lot of people were milling around on the porch. No kids our age. And the music drifting outside was definitely not the kind we usually listened to.

"Do we want to do the dance?" I asked.

"I'm kinda wiped out," Tara said. "And I'm more interested in the sleigh ride. Dances I can go to at home. But a sleigh ride . . ."

"Okay, go do the sleigh ride."

"*Go do?* You're coming with us."

"I'm really in the mood to walk."

"Then we'll walk with you."

"Tara, don't be silly. You're right. You may never get a chance to do this again. So do it now. With Shaun. I'm just going to walk."

"If you're sure . . ."

I could see how badly she wanted to do it. And I couldn't blame her.

"A hundred percent," I said.

Shaun paid the driver—I guess with his reserved money—at the front of the line. Then he and Tara climbed into the sleigh. The driver tucked a thick blanket over their laps.

Tara looked so happy. When it came to revealing his emotions, Shaun might be a flatliner, but he'd obviously managed to win Tara over big-time.

The driver slapped the reins over the backs of the horses and they took off, little bells attached to the reins jingling as they disappeared around the corner. I thought I saw Shaun lean in to kiss Tara—or maybe she leaned in to kiss him. But either way, I knew romantic-at-heart Tara was going to get a sleigh ride she'd never forget.

By the time I got home I was coooold!

I could smell something spicy coming from the kitchen. When I walked in, Mom was sitting at the table, making notes in a binder. She was wearing velour lounging pants and a tank top. Her fuzzy socked feet were on a chair.

"Hi, sweetie," she said. "I made some tension-reducing tea. It has chamomile. No caffeine. It'll warm you and help you sleep."

How had she known that I'd be so tense I was close to snapping in two?

"Why would I need help sleeping?" I mumbled as I poured myself a cup. I sat down across from Mom. "Are you tense?"

She laughed lightly. "No, but I don't believe a person can ever be too relaxed."

I took off my gloves and wrapped my hands around the mug.

"I made some spice cake, too," she said.

"You've been busy. I thought you were going on the Victorian Walk."

"I did. I have lots of ideas now for decorating. I wanted to write them all down while they were fresh in my mind."

"You didn't go to the dance?"

She took a sip of tea and shook her head. "No, maybe next year. What did you think of the houses?"

"I think they're officially called cottages."

"I think you're right. Did you see the Wynters'?" she asked.

"Yeah, it was pretty awesome."

"I thought so, too."

She went back to scribbling in her binder.

"Mom, can I ask you a question?"

She looked up at me and smiled. "Of course, sweetie."

I was starting to get warm and thought about taking off my parka, but I felt a little silly talking to my mom about a serious subject when I was wearing a Victorian costume. It wasn't me. My parka was. And what I wanted to ask . . . well, I wanted honesty.

"Is Marsha the reason you and Dad got a divorce?"

Her mouth dropped open slightly. Then she

reached across the table and took my hand. "Oh, honey, no."

"Then why?"

"Oh, Ashleigh, your dad and I were barely eighteen when we got married. We had so much growing up and changing to do, and we didn't realize then that we'd change in different directions. Your dad likes the big corporate world and travel and schmoozing and entertaining people. Me"—she shrugged—"I like the simple, small-town life. Your dad and I still love each other, and we want each other to be happy. And we admitted that the best way to be happy was not to be together."

"So you just gave up?"

"We recognized that we wanted—needed—different things to be happy. Your dad needed someone who loves the glamorous world he lives in. And I needed something else. I'm not exactly sure what it is yet. I'm still trying to figure that out. Most girls figure it out in their twenties. But I was busy being a mommy and a wife."

"Are you saying you don't know who you are?"

"Pretty much, yeah."

I slumped back in my chair. I hardly knew what to say. You don't expect your mom to have an identity crisis. She's the adult. She's . . . well, she's your *mom*! If she didn't know who she was, how would you ever know?

I leaned forward. "Do you like Mr. Wynter?"

"Of course I do." Her eyes widened. "Oh, no, not like what you're thinking. He's just a friend. I'm in no hurry for romance, but if I were, well . . ."

Her cheeks turned red, and she began drawing hearts on a page in her binder. Hearts, like I did whenever I started crushing on a guy and wondering what going on a date with him would be like.

That was just too weird to even think about.

It was a little after midnight when Tara crept into my room. I'd been sitting on the window seat, looking out onto the street so I'd seen the sleigh arrive. I'd heard her laugh as the driver helped her get out. I'd watched as Shaun put his arms around her and rubbed his nose against hers while the sleigh went up the street. I had looked away when he'd kissed her.

"Oh, you're awake," she said as she closed the door behind her.

The only light I'd left on was the lamp beside my bed. I'd put a silk scarf over it so the room looked a little blue. I didn't think it would have looked like much light from the street. If she would have even noticed. She'd obviously been totally caught up in Shaun. Which I completely understood. I might not get the attraction of Shaun, but I knew when I was ready to have a boyfriend, I'd want to be immersed in him too.

And I definitely would be, if he took me on a romantic sleigh ride.

"You're only here for one more day," I told her. "You didn't really think I was going to spend what little time we had left sleeping, did you?"

I helped her get out of her Victorian costume. When she was in her flannel PJ's, we both sat on the window seat—it was that big—looking out, with my grandma's quilt wrapped around both of us.

"I kinda like it here, Ash," Tara said.

"Yeah, it definitely has its moments."

"Shaun and I are talking about coming back during spring break."

"That'd be great."

"And probably in the summer. Maybe we could get summer jobs here, working for your mom."

"Please do," I said. "You can make the breakfast *and* beds, while I sleep in."

"Think of all the different kinds of people you'll meet. I think it'll be fun."

It would be fun. Especially if Tara was here.

We were quiet for a few minutes, watching snowflakes fall.

"If Josh didn't have a girlfriend," she said quietly, "wouldn't you go out with him more than once?"

I nodded. "Twice at least."

"How could you not want him to be your boyfriend?"

"Love doesn't last when you're young, so why bother acting like it does?"

I was staring hard out the window because it had been difficult saying that. Especially to Tara, who thought Shaun was her forever guy. I just didn't get it.

Tara was so quiet that I was afraid I'd hurt her feelings. Having a boyfriend was the one thing we'd never agreed on.

Twisting my head slightly, I rested my cheek on my upturned knees and looked at Tara. "Do you really think you and Shaun will live happily ever after?"

"I don't know, Ash. I just know that I'm happy now."

"It'll hurt so much if you break up."

"What if we never break up?"

"Then I guess you'll have happily ever after."

"Exactly."

She looked really pleased with herself. Really happy. But it was scary to think of happily ever after. It was scary to think about trusting someone enough to give him your heart now, hoping he wouldn't break it later.

18

As Tara explained it, from the time they'd arrived on the island, it had been all about what Tara wanted to do. Hang with me. Eat fudge. Dress in Victorian clothes. Eat fudge. Take a sleigh ride.

So their last day on the island was all about what Shaun wanted to do. And he wanted to go to the mainland. He wanted to drive across the bridge connecting the straits.

Why he thought that would be a rush, I don't know. Had to be a guy thing.

I'd stopped trying to figure Shaun out. He made Tara happy and that was all that mattered. And he was willing to include me in this little excursion across the water, and that made me happy.

I hadn't been on the ferry or to the mainland yet, so I was excited about getting to tag along. I wasn't even thinking about being the odd number.

And I didn't even complain that it felt like the temperature had dropped a hundred degrees since yesterday.

Shaun, with his love of numbers, would have no doubt spent time explaining that my theory was impossible. But I was beginning to learn the difference between very cold and realllly cold.

Shaun was also very methodical. He had the entire day planned out. But he was being secretive and wouldn't show Tara the list on his PDA. Yes, his list. He was going to check them off as we did them. Geeky. But again, he made Tara happy, so I was okay with it.

"Please, tell me just one thing we're going to do," Tara begged as we trudged to the dock. She was hanging on to his arm, which was a good thing because the wind was strong today.

"We're going to drive across the bridge."

I wasn't sure how we were going to do that. I figured he was going to rent a car. If they had a car rental place over there. Surely they did.

"I know *that*," Tara said. "Tell me something else."

"Have lunch."

She laughed. I didn't know why. Love did strange things to people.

The ferry horn blasted.

"Come on, we better hurry," I said.

We practically ran to the dock, bought our tickets, and dashed onto the ferry. We went inside where the wind couldn't hit us. It wasn't much warmer. I was concentrating on figuring out where the warmest seat might be when I heard Shaun say, "Hey," greeting someone.

But who did Shaun know here?

I spun around and watched as Josh approached from the rear of the cabin, or whatever they called the little room on top of the ferry. It had big windows so we'd have a great view.

Josh and Shaun tapped knuckles.

"Thanks for doing this, man," Shaun said.

"Not a problem," Josh said.

"Doing what?" I asked.

"Josh has a car. He's going to drive us over the bridge."

"Oh, that's nice of him," Tara said.

But her tone sounded funny, like someone who's trying to appear surprised but isn't.

"Yeah, it is," I said. And I was back to thinking that being a third wheel wouldn't have been nearly as awkward.

Maybe I should get off now, before things get any worse.

The ferry horn sounded again, and the boat

began to move away from the dock.

Too late. I'm stuck.

"Cool. Let's watch," Shaun said, taking Tara's hand and pulling her toward a window.

Which, of course, left me standing there with Josh.

"You didn't know I was going to be here," he said.

I shook my head.

He nodded.

"Where's Nathalie?" I asked.

"Working."

He shoved his hands into his pockets. I was still cold. I wanted to reach out and button up his jacket, like I thought bundling up someone else would help warm me.

"This"—I pointed my fingers at him, pointed them at me, pointed them at him—"is not a date."

"I know. Shaun needed a car. I've got a car."

"And no experience driving it."

He grinned. "I've got experience."

"We'll see."

"Ash, come see the view," Tara called out.

How touristy. A few other people were on the ferry, and they all looked at me. I rolled my eyes and grumbled, "She's the fudgie, not me."

But I did walk over to the window and looked

out. It appeared to be as snowy on the mainland as it was on the island.

I felt Josh come up behind me.

"You're shivering," he said.

He got nearer. Put his arms around me. I knew it was impossible, bundled up like I was, but I swear I could feel his warmth. It felt so good. I knew I should shove him away, or at least step away, but I didn't.

I just stood there and let him hold me. And watched the mainland grow closer and closer.

And kept telling myself that this wouldn't be a date. I wouldn't be the other woman. He was a guy, I was a girl. We were friends. It was no big deal. We needed his car.

Unfortunately, I was also feeling like maybe I needed him, too.

The city on the mainland was bigger than the one on the island, but it still had a historic feel to it. A lot of the stores looked like lodges and had fireplaces. We decided to eat at a restaurant in a log cabin. Josh explained to the hostess that his friends were from the South, not used to the cold, and asked if she'd give us a table by the fireplace.

We had to wait ten minutes for one to open up, but it was so worth it. I was actually able to take off my jacket and gloves. I kept my knitted cap on, trying to retain any heat my body might absorb from the fire.

After we'd given the waitress our order, Tara said, "I know this is supposed to be your day, Shaun, but there are so many little shops—"

Shaun gave her a quick kiss.

No doubt to shut her up. What guy wanted to spend *his* day shopping?

He pulled his PDA out of his jacket pocket and started tapping the stylus against it. Then he showed it to Tara.

She gave a little squeal before looking at me with a huge smile. "Number one on his list of things to do is 'Let Tara shop.'"

Squeezing his arm, she kissed him.

Okay, so maybe I was starting to get the attraction to Shaun. His idea of having a great time seemed to be making sure that Tara was happy.

I glanced over at Josh. "Did you know about the shopping?"

"Nah, but I'm cool with it."

Lunch was tasty, but when we were finished, I sorta hated to leave the warmth of the fireplace. I prolonged it as long as I could by ordering dessert: apple cobbler. But I skipped the à la mode part. I couldn't believe the waitress had even asked if I wanted ice cream.

Then she looked at Josh and winked. "Two spoons?"

"Sure," he said, like we were a couple, used to sharing.

I would have protested, but it seemed petty. Besides, Tara and Shaun were sharing.

When I saw how large the bowls were, I was glad I had someone to help me eat it. It was scrumptious with a lot of brown sugar crumbs. And it was hot. Anything hot was good.

Which meant Josh was good. I nearly choked with that thought.

He looked up at me. "You okay?"

"I'm fine."

"You mind sharing the cobbler?"

"No, not at all."

"Thanks. I could die from boredom shopping, so this could be my last meal."

Grinning, I tapped my spoon against the side of the bowl. "You worry a lot about last meals."

"Hey, you never know."

"Actually, I do know. You're not going to die from boredom."

I dipped out some cobbler. Some of the melted butter and sugar dripped on my chin. I wiped at it with my napkin.

"You missed some," Josh said.

He grazed his thumb near the corner of my mouth. I swallowed hard. It didn't mean anything, I told myself. So why did my toes curl?

"There," he said.

And while I was still recovering from his touch, he finished off the cobbler, looking smug.

I wanted to accuse him of distracting me on purpose, but that would mean acknowledging that he had the power to distract me. As a rule, guys didn't distract me. They interested me . . . *if* I wanted to be interested.

With Josh, I always felt like I had no control.

Once we finished dessert, I couldn't put it off any longer. We paid for our meal, bundled up, and strolled through a square that had all kinds of shops. I was very aware that Tara and Shaun were holding hands, while Josh and I weren't.

At one point my gloved hand bumped up against his and I jumped. It was embarrassing. I could watch a horror movie without closing my eyes, but I was all jumpy just walking with a guy. It made no sense.

"So." Josh cleared his throat as we walked along the cobblestone pavement. "You and Chase. I guess you've run your course."

I peered over at him. "What?"

He held up a bare finger. Why didn't he need gloves? "Date one, the hayride. Date two, V.P. And you're a two-date girl, right?"

"Usually, yeah. But I'm not sure V.P. really counted, since I spent more time visiting with Tara than I did with Chase. And he and Shaun were palling around, so if he asks, I'll go out with him again."

"You would?"

Would I?

"Yeah, probably," I said.

"You really like him?"

"I like him," I clarified. "He gets the whole not-wanting-to-date-the-same-person-over-and-over thing."

"Yeah, but doesn't that limit . . ." His voice trailed off.

"Limit what?"

He cleared his throat again. "The first time you kiss someone it's kinda awkward. So isn't your life just filled with awkward first kisses?"

"You and I weren't awkward."

The words popped out before I could stop them. Ours had been so not awkward—at least not until I realized I was suddenly the other woman.

"No," he said, and his gaze dropped to my lips, which made them do that whole irritating tingling thing. "It wasn't."

His voice had gone deep like he might be strangling. He cleared his throat again. Maybe he was coming down with whatever Nathalie had been sick with.

"Hey, guys!" Tara called out. "There's a mirror maze over here. Shaun wants to go through it. You wanna come?"

"Sure," Josh said, taking my hand before I could respond. "It'll be fun."

I wasn't sure if his taking my hand was calculated or done without thought. But it seemed right as we headed to the building. Only when we got there, we saw that it was closed. The sign said they were only open May through October.

"That sucks!" Shaun exclaimed.

Who'd have thought he'd get emotional over mirrors?

"We'll come back in the summer," Tara said.

How could she be so sure they'd still be together come summer?

Nodding, Shaun drew her up against his side. "Sounds like a plan, babe."

He sounded equally certain. I just couldn't fathom that.

For the first time in my life, I felt a flicker of regret that I'd been so insistent on not having a boyfriend. I had no one to make plans with for next week, much less next summer.

"You okay?" Josh asked.

"Oh, yeah, I'm just sorry it's closed."

"Well, maybe we—" He stopped. Swallowed. "Maybe when they come back, you can go with them."

And I knew then he'd been about to say that he and I could come back sometime. Before he'd remembered that we couldn't. That I wouldn't.

"Have you ever been inside?"

"Oh, yeah. It's pretty awesome."

We all started walking around again, but Josh didn't let go of my hand. And while I knew that I should pull free, I didn't.

It was a couple of hours before we walked to the public garage where Josh kept his car. And—it was a red Ford Mustang.

"Are you okay?" he asked.

He seemed to be asking me that a lot today, but then I realized that my hand was aching from squeezing his so tightly.

"It's my favorite kind of car," I admitted. "And my favorite color."

"Mine, too. On both counts. It was an early graduation present from Dad, which really puts the pressure on me now to graduate."

"Is there a chance you won't?"

He grinned. "Nah."

"You'd better drive it carefully," I said.

He gave me a really hot grin. "Careful is boring."

Tara and Shaun climbed into the back and I slid into the passenger seat. I took off my glove and ran my hand over the dash. Then I buckled up and listened to the car purr as Josh revved up the engine.

But it was just for show.

Once he started to back out, he did drive carefully. Mainly because the streets were slick. I was surprised that the bridge was open for traffic. Only a few cars were out, so I relaxed and enjoyed the ride.

It had begun to grow dark already. The bridge lights came on as we were driving over it. It was beautiful from a distance, but amazing up close. When we got back to Chateau Ashleigh, I was going to have to thank Shaun for this day.

"Winter's the worst time to drive around, but any other season, it's great. And each season is so different," Josh said. "Maybe sometime . . ."

He left it unfinished, but I knew what he'd been about to say. That dangling date thing again. A date that would never happen, because he had a girlfriend.

I didn't answer. I don't know why. Maybe I didn't want to completely destroy the possibility that someday we might take another drive together.

19

It was harder than I thought it would be to watch Tara leave the next morning. Before the Wynters had arrived at the house to begin work, Tara, Shaun, and I took a taxi to the airport. While Shaun went to check in their bags, I asked Tara something I hadn't been in the mood to know the answer to last night.

"Going to the mainland, driving across the bridge, that wasn't Shaun's idea, was it?"

"He mentioned he wanted to do it."

She looked guilty.

"Okay, inviting Josh . . . Shaun's idea?"

She scrunched up her face. "Let's just say, Shaun knew he'd be interested, and I knew you'd have a good time with him. And we did need someone with a car."

"He has a girlfriend."

Tara looked at the ground.

"Tara?"

She lifted her gaze to mine. "Shaun told me something but I can't tell you. It's a guy to girl-friend thing. Just . . . just don't count yesterday out as a date."

"What are you talking about?"

She opened her mouth, but before she could say anything, Shaun returned.

"Hey, babe, the puddle-jumper's ready for us."

She laughed nervously. "That's what he calls the small planes."

I wasn't sure if she was nervous about flying or nervous because she'd almost gotten caught telling me something she wasn't supposed to. And I probably wouldn't know until she got home tonight, and I could call her when Shaun wasn't around.

I gave her a tight hug. "Thanks so much for coming."

I even hugged Shaun. I had a feeling I needed to thank him for something, but I wasn't exactly sure what.

I stayed and watched until the plane lifted into the sky.

Then I rode the taxi back to Chateau Ashleigh, paid the driver, and got out. I had to admit it was kinda cool to travel over the snow, to have a place that looked so peaceful. And I was getting used to the quiet. The island was almost beginning to feel familiar. And after having my best friend here for a few days, our cottage was actually starting to feel like . . . home.

I opened the gate, took a step, and—

Bam!

Something hit me in the side of the head.

Rubbing my head, I turned slightly. Nathalie was standing there with a red, red nose and red eyes. What was up with that?

Corey and Shanna were with her. I guess they'd been hiding behind a tree or a mound of snow or something. I hadn't seen them when I arrived.

"I've never been in a snowball fight," I said smiling, walking toward them. "Are there rules?"

"You bitch!" Nathalie yelled. "You think I don't know you're the reason my boyfriend broke up with me?"

"Josh broke up with you?"

She nodded her head so fast that I was surprised it didn't fly off.

I had a lot more questions, but when three girls start pelting you with snowballs—and they're way more experienced at it than you are—talking is the last thing on your mind.

Running is the first.

And run I did. Straight into the house.

"This island isn't big enough for the both of us!" Nathalie yelled after me.

Did she really just say that?

Breathing heavily, I slammed the door closed behind me.

Was that what Tara had known? The guy code that had become a guy-girlfriend code? That Josh was going to break up with Nathalie?

And I was the reason?

I was scared. Did he expect me to become his girlfriend now?

I wasn't going to do that, no matter how much I liked him. I wasn't ready for a boyfriend. I wasn't ready for that whole clingy he-is-my-world kind of thing.

I heard Mom's laughter floating out from the kitchen, followed by Mr. Wynter's. That meant Josh was here.

I dashed up the stairs and found him painting another guestroom, his back to me.

"You broke up with Nathalie?" I demanded.

Holding the paint roller, he turned from the wall. He didn't deny it, and I didn't really need to hear his answer. The answer was a shattered snowball caught inside the collar of my coat and sliding down my back and sending shivers up my spine. "What did you tell her? She hates me. She thinks I'm the reason that you broke up with her."

Shaking his head, he rolled his eyes with obvious exasperation—only I didn't know if it was at me or at her.

"I didn't tell her that," he said.

"What did you say?"

He set the paint roller aside and took a step toward me. I held up my hand to stop him.

"You're shivering," he said. "We need to get you in front of a fire."

And it was a little difficult to be indignant when my teeth were chattering, but still I managed. "They threw snowballs at me."

"Who did?"

I shook my head. I hadn't meant to tell him. I didn't want him mad at her. I just wanted him to fix things.

"Nathalie?" he asked.

"It doesn't matter."

"I explained everything to her last night. I never mentioned you. I'll go talk to her again."

"You're not the one who needs to talk to her." I took out my cell phone. "What's Chase's number?"

He gave it to me. I punched it in, stored it.

"Why do you need to call him?" Josh asked, and I thought I heard jealousy in his voice.

"Because he likes Nathalie."

"Really?"

I nodded. "Just something he said about you claiming her and never giving another guy a chance. I don't know." I shrugged. "I think that's the reason he dates so many girls. Because the one he wanted wasn't available."

Josh remained silent.

"I hate being the reason you broke up with her," I said.

"You're not the reason."

I gave him a hard stare.

"Okay, I guess in a way you are."

In a way? In the only way possible. *Just call me Homewrecker.*

"I'm not going to date you, Josh."

"Look, I know you think, new girl in town so I dump old girlfriend. But that's not how it is. Do you know how I became her boyfriend?"

I shook my head.

He gave me a wry grin. "I'm twelve, she's eleven. She passes a note to me in class. Will you be my boyfriend? And there were two little boxes. Yes. No."

"Like that George Strait song?"

"Not exactly, but close enough. Like I said. I was twelve. What did I know? I checked yes. And

I've been her boyfriend ever since."

"Because of a note?" I asked incredulously.

"Pretty much. You know how Nathalie is. Once she started telling people I was her boyfriend, it seemed mean to say I wasn't. And yeah, I'm a jerk." He closed his eyes. "It was easier to be her boyfriend than try to break up with her. And I liked her." He opened his eyes. "But not the way I like you."

"So I *am* the reason you broke up."

"Only because you made me realize that it wasn't fair to either Nathalie or me for us to keep going together. She deserves someone who *really* likes her, who wants to be with her because he doesn't want to be with anyone else."

I thought about the conversation I'd had with Mom. If she and Dad had waited a few years, would they have gotten married at all?

"And you're not that guy."

He looked a little sad. "I'm definitely not that guy."

"It doesn't matter. I don't want a boyfriend."

I turned on my heel and hurried to my room. Shedding my coat and hat, I flopped onto my bed.

I was scared, so scared. Not horror-movie scared. But real-life scared.

I wouldn't go out with Josh, even if he asked.

Maybe he wouldn't ask. *Please don't ask.*

Because one date wouldn't be enough. I was afraid a hundred dates wouldn't be enough.

And then I'd have a boyfriend. Until someone else moved to the island and he broke my heart.

I took out my cell phone and called Chase. At least one person on this island would be happy.

Later that night, after I was certain she was back home, I called Tara.

"You knew he was going to break up with her," I said without preamble.

She groaned. "Yeah, sorta. The guy-code stuff? He'd asked Shaun for tips on how to break up with a girl so that they stayed friends."

"Well, he sure blew that. Anyway, how would Shaun know?"

"There are a lot of breakups around here. He's heard things. Guys talk."

"Guy code," I grumbled.

"Yeah. So when are you and Josh going out?"

"We're not."

"Why not?"

I clearly heard the disbelief in her voice.

"We're just not."

"It's because you like him so much and you're afraid one or two dates won't be enough."

The problem with having a best friend was that she knew me a little too well. But there was more to it. I didn't want to hurt Nathalie. While she was sometimes a little out there, she had made me feel welcome and part of the island.

"You're *afraid* you'll want him to be your boyfriend," she continued. "You're afraid you'll betray this pact you made with yourself to never have one."

"I didn't make a pact to *never* have one. I just made a pact not to have one until I was way older."

"Dammit, Ash."

Tara never cursed, so I knew she was really upset with me. Well, welcome to the club. If she was still here, she'd probably be throwing snowballs at me too.

"He's a nice guy," Tara said.

"So is Chase."

"Do you think about Chase all the time?"

"What's that got to do with anything?"

"You're hopeless."

No, I was scared. Scared she was right about everything.

20

The next two days were hell. Mostly because I didn't want to run into Josh, so I got out of bed way too early and headed down to the kitchen to grab a cup of coffee. I was nestled safely in my room, with no plans to come out, by the time I heard activity downstairs.

I finished designing the website, and I decided now was as good a time as any to begin working on my novel. Maybe if I killed off a few fictitious people I'd feel better. After a day and a half, I'd typed, "Chapter One." Which I thought was a pretty good beginning.

Where to go from there, though, was a mystery.

I was sitting at the computer staring out the window—thinking about Josh, not the story—when someone knocked. It was Mom, and she looked worried.

"Are you all right?"

"Oh, yeah." I pointed to the computer screen. "I'm working on my novel."

She was holding a small package, but she still managed to cross her arms over her chest. "You're not avoiding someone?"

I shook my head.

She narrowed her eyes. "Okay, if you're sure. But if you are avoiding someone, he's left for the day."

"I'm not."

But I was glad to know he was no longer there.

She set the package on the desk. "This came for you."

I knew what it was.

"Thanks."

She studied me for a minute. "Tomorrow, Mr. Wynter and I are going to the mainland to look at some different wallpapering. Josh is taking the day off, so you'll be here all alone. Will you be okay with that, or do you want to come with us?"

"I'm a big girl. I'm okay with that."

I couldn't be sure, but I thought Mom looked relieved. She headed for the door.

"Mom?"

She stopped with her hand on the doorknob and looked back at me.

"Mom, I'm really confused about when you

know whether or not a guy should be your boyfriend."

"Don't think about it so much, Ashleigh. It's not something your head decides."

"Do you think you'll ever have a boyfriend again?"

"I hope so."

"But aren't you afraid of getting hurt again?"

I thought I saw tears glisten in her eyes. "You know, Ashleigh, some of my very best memories include moments spent with your dad. Yes, it hurt when we split, but what we had for a while made the hurt worth it."

When Mom left, I sat for a long time thinking about what she'd said. Then I called Dad.

"You know, we actually had some snow flurries today," he said. "I thought of you."

"I've been thinking of you, too, but not because of the snow. I . . ." Gosh, this was hard, and I realized that Josh breaking up with Nathalie had probably been a lot harder for him than just staying with her would have been. That it took a lot of guts to admit a mistake and do something about it. "I was mad at you, mad about Marsha."

"I know."

"I just . . . I didn't understand everything, I guess. Anyway, I thought maybe I could come spend spring break with you."

"We'd like that."

"Will you tell Marsha that I'll be one of her bridesmaids?"

"I sure will. That'll make her very happy."

Strangely, I thought it would probably make Mom happy too.

Dad and I talked for a while longer. I didn't tell him about Josh because I didn't know what was going to happen with us. And I figured he'd fly up to check him out. I wasn't ready for that. I figured Josh wouldn't be, either.

After we hung up, I decided I needed to do one more thing. I opened the box Mom had brought up. Inside was another little box. It contained an eggling. Tara had given me one as a going-away present before I left Texas. Last night I'd gone online and ordered one for Nathalie—a peace offering, even though I wasn't the one who started the war. I dropped it into a little gift bag and stuffed tissue around it. I bundled up.

Maybe it was because I'd been inside for two days, but it seemed a lot colder as I trudged to Sweet Temptations. I'd given Nathalie's situation a lot of thought, and I'd decided that if she really loved Josh, she'd have fought for him. And that she would have called him by name instead of by label. For her, it was all about having *a boyfriend*. Not the right boyfriend.

Still, this island was my home now. It had to be big enough for the two of us.

"I've got to check on something in the back room," she said as soon as I walked in.

"Wait," I said. "We need to talk."

"If you want to talk, talk to my boyfriend."

"Look, about Josh—"

"Not Josh. Chase."

I must have had a confused look on my face, because she rolled her eyes.

"Chase is my boyfriend now."

I looked at Chase. Folding his arms on top of the counter, he grinned.

"Wow. That was quick," I said.

"Not really," Nathalie said. Her voice was sharp, impatient. "He's liked me for a long time and I liked him. It's just that I had a boyfriend. Until you came to town."

"So we owe you big-time," Chase said. "How about a pound of free fudge?"

"We agreed you'd stop giving away free fudge," Nathalie said.

"We agreed I'd stop giving away free fudge to get dates." He winked at her, then turned his attention back to me. "So what do you want?"

"Actually, I do need to ship some fudge, but I have to talk to Nathalie first."

"I've got nothing to say to you," she said.

I walked over to where she stood and set the bag on the counter. "This is for you."

She looked at it like it might suddenly transform into a monster. "What is it?"

"Look inside."

She took out the box. "An eggling? What's that?"

"It's a tiny little garden. You crack the top and water what's inside. And it grows a little plant so you'll have spring before spring."

"Oh, cool." She looked at me. "So why are you giving it to me?"

"Because you're my friend. And I didn't mean for you to get hurt."

"He said you weren't the reason, but if you weren't the reason, then I was the reason." Tears welled in her eyes. "I didn't want to be the reason."

"Sometimes, no one is the reason. It just happens. It happened with my parents. That's why we moved here."

"It hurt."

"I know. And I'm sorry."

She leaned toward me and said in a low voice, "I was afraid if Josh wasn't my boyfriend that I wouldn't have one, and I really wanted to have a boyfriend. But I like Chase more. I just didn't know it until he came over and we started talking to each other."

"I'm glad it worked out."

And I was. She'd thought having a boyfriend was more important than who the boyfriend was. So it was good that Josh had broken up with her.

"So I guess we just switched boyfriends," Nathalie said.

"Not really. I mean, Chase was never my boyfriend and Josh . . . well, I'm not dating him."

"Why not?" She looked completely baffled. So did Chase.

I swallowed hard, trying to decide if I should tell her the truth.

"I don't think I'm ready to have a boyfriend, and if I go out with him, I don't think one date will be enough."

"How will you know if you don't go out with him?"

"Good question."

"You should at least go out with him once."

"You think?"

She nodded. "When I'm not mad at him anymore, I can write a recommendation letter."

Which would no doubt contain way too much information.

"That's okay. It's probably best to just stumble along on my own."

"Whatever." She held up the box. "Thanks for the eggling."

I smiled. "Maybe in a couple of weeks, you, Corey, and Shanna could come to my house for a sleepover."

"Oh, yeah, that'd be fun."

"Great." I turned to Chase. "Guess I'm ready to send that fudge now."

"To Tara?" he asked.

"No, to my future stepmom. Her name is Marsha."

"All right, then, fill this out." Chase snatched up the order form and wrote something on it. Then he passed it to me. "And I'll take care of it for you."

In the bottom corner, he'd written, "Thanks," and drawn a smiley face. I'd never known a guy who drew smiley faces.

He seemed so happy. I started filling out the form.

I guess he'd known Nathalie long enough to know what he was getting into.

21

The next morning, I slept late, snuggled beneath the blankets, relishing the warmth my body created. No one to avoid today, no reason to get up before the crack of dawn to grab my coffee.

I was vaguely aware of Mom peeking into my room to say good-bye. I remember peering out from beneath the covers and thinking it wasn't even dawn yet, it was still so dark.

The final time I opened my eyes, I thought maybe I'd slept all day. It was really shadowy in the room. Wrapping my blankets around me, because they still held warmth, I shuffled over to the window. The sky was gray. The leafless branches were swaying. I could see white caps in the distance on the lake. And snow. A lot of snow. Blizzard snow.

Oh my gosh! Were we in the middle of a storm?

Ugh! I didn't want to think about all the snow

I'd have to shovel—unless Josh would do it. Maybe he would. Or not.

I sat on the window seat and tried not to think about him, but he was all I thought about. All I dreamed about too. I thought if I just avoided him that I'd forget about him.

But all it did was make me miss him and want him around more.

By late afternoon, the snow was coming down more heavily.

Mom called to say that the ferry couldn't run and that she and Mr. Wynter were going to have to stay on the mainland. That I was going to be on my own until the weather cleared—probably sometime tomorrow. I assured her that I was fine being alone and told her not to worry. Then I checked the locks on all the doors and windows—and wished the house didn't creak so much. I lit the fire in the parlor fireplace and wished I had someone to snuggle with, because a snowstorm just seemed like good cuddling weather.

Night had fallen, and I was in the kitchen making a yummy peanut butter and jelly sandwich when I heard the doorbell. I jumped and my heart gave a little kick. This was so a horror-movie scene—bad weather, and a girl cut off from the outside world.

Only killers didn't usually ring the doorbell.

Still, I opened a drawer and took out the meat cleaver Mom used for cutting chicken. The doorbell rang again and kept ringing.

"All right already," I muttered as I hurried down the hallway.

I hesitated when I saw a large shadowy form behind the etched-glass window of the door. I'd turned on the porch light, and whoever was there blocked most of it.

"Ashleigh!" The figure banged on the door and I nearly dropped the cleaver.

Josh. My beating heart should have returned to a normal speed, but it didn't. I wasn't ready to face him yet. I jerked open the door. "What?"

Covered in frost and snow, he edged past me. "Geez, it's cold out there."

"And you just brought the cold inside." I shut the door. "What are you doing here?"

"My dad called and—what the hell is that?"

He pointed to the cleaver.

I angled my chin. "I was in the middle of cutting my peanut butter and jelly sandwich."

"With a meat cleaver?"

"It's quick and makes a perfectly straight cut."

He grinned. "Yeah, right. You've obviously watched too many movies. Who'd you think I was? Freddy Krueger?"

"What are you doing here?" I repeated, not in the mood for his sarcasm or teasing. Plus I was feeling a little silly holding my weapon of choice.

"Like I said, my dad called. The ferry shut down before they could get back. I decided to check to make sure that you were okay."

"Why wouldn't I be okay?"

"The storms here can get pretty intense, and if you've never been through one"—he dropped his gaze back to the cleaver—"I just thought you might get freaked if you were all alone."

It was nice of him to worry about me but totally unnecessary.

I sighed. "I'm fine, thanks. You can go back home now."

"You're kidding, right? Did you not look out there?"

"It's snowing."

"It's a blizzard. I'm not going back out."

"You're not staying here."

He raised an eyebrow. "This is an inn."

"Not yet. We're not officially open for business."

"Tough. It's easy to get disoriented out there. Last year a guy froze to death three feet from his front porch."

"Call a taxi."

The other eyebrow shot up. "Is this any way to thank me for showing concern?"

"You know, I think you probably came over here because *you* were afraid to be alone."

"I really did want to make sure you were okay."

"You could have called."

"It's not the same."

I didn't want to admit to him that a little part of me was glad not to be alone anymore. Because the wind was loud and now that it was night, it was scary.

"Oh, all right." Besides, if the ferry wasn't running, the taxi probably wasn't either. "Come on. I'll split my sandwich with you."

"I make a mean grilled cheese sandwich, and I'm really in the mood for something warm."

We went to the kitchen. I got out everything he'd need to make the sandwiches. After I fixed us some hot chocolate, I leaned against the counter and watched as he buttered bread and dropped it onto the heated skillet. He topped it with cheese and another slice of buttered bread.

He slid a spatula beneath the grilling bread, lifted it slightly, and peeked beneath it. He dropped it back into place.

"You've been avoiding me," he said, talking to the sandwich.

I laughed. He looked over at me. "Sorry. I just realized that you talk to a lot of inanimate objects."

"I'm just keeping an eye on it so it doesn't burn."

"If you say so."

"Soooo," he said.

I shrugged. "Soooo?"

"You've been avoiding me."

Taking a sip of hot chocolate, I peered at him over the rim of my mug. "Yeah."

"Why?"

"It just seemed simpler."

He flipped the sandwich over. It sizzled. "Simpler or safer?"

"Both."

He took the sandwich out of the skillet and cut it in half, placing each half on a plate. He carried it to the table while I took the mugs over.

"Where do you want to sit?" he asked.

"Doesn't matter."

Suddenly everything went dark. The house was almost solid black and so, so quiet.

To my mortification, I released a tiny squeal like a terrified mouse.

"Shh. It's okay. Power just went out. Happens all the time when we get a storm like this. Where are the flashlights?"

"I don't know," I whispered.

"What do you mean you don't know?"

"I mean, I. Don't. Know. We haven't even unpacked everything yet."

"That's the first thing I'd unpack."

Had to be a guy thing. "Yeah, well, sorry, but we didn't."

"Candles?"

"I have some in my room."

I heard him release a deep sigh. "Okay."

Suddenly the faintest hint of light spilled out, and I realized he'd opened his cell phone. "I'll see if I can find those candles."

"I'll go with you."

"Why are you whispering?"

"You're supposed to whisper when the lights go out."

"So the boogeyman doesn't get you?"

I shoved on his arm. "Let's just go get the candles."

Clinging to the sleeve of his jacket, I followed him through the house. A cell phone doesn't produce a huge amount of light. But I guess our eyes were adjusting, because we didn't run into anything.

I directed him toward my desk, where I had the candle that sounded like a crackling fire when it burned. I lit it. Amazing how much light a candle could make. And how eerie it really made things when it was flickering and was the only light. I lit another one that he'd be able to carry easily downstairs. Then I began packing additional candles in a tote bag I had. We'd probably get nauseous sniffing all the various scents.

"Hey, come here," Josh said.

He was sitting on the love seat looking out the window.

"What is it?" I asked, walking over. "The lights are out. You can't see anything out there."

"I know." He wrapped his hand around my arm and pulled me down until I was nestled between his thighs, my back to his chest. "I just wanted to hold you."

Deep down, I knew I should have been mad about being manipulated, but I just couldn't seem to work up the anger. The truth was I wanted him to hold me, too. He nuzzled the back of my neck. And, of course, my toes curled.

"You think our parents are okay?" I asked.

"Yeah, if you look in the distance, you can make out the lights on the mainland. They're fine."

"I'm sorry your dad got stuck over there, just because Mom wanted to look at wallpaper."

"He won't mind. I think he likes your mom. He mentioned something about taking her to a movie."

It was a weird thought: Mom with a guy who wasn't my dad.

His arms tightened around me. "Want to hear something silly?"

"Yeah, I could use a laugh."

"I've never asked a girl out."

Okay, I didn't laugh. Not even a snicker.

"I don't know how to do it," Josh continued. "I've spent the past two days trying to figure out what to say."

I shifted around slightly. "You and Nathalie didn't date?"

"We went out, but I never really asked her if she wanted to. I mean, there was never any question that she'd say yes. We were 'together,' so if one of us wanted to do something, the other went along."

I thought of Tara just handing Shaun her fudge or dragging him through a bunch of little shops when he had no interest in them. Or maybe he had. Again, with him it was hard to tell. But she never actually asked him if he wanted to go. She wanted to go, so he went along.

"Did Nathalie ever call you by your name?"

He chuckled quietly and the sound vibrated near my ear. "You know, I never noticed until you pointed it out how she always referred to me as her boyfriend. I know I'm not arm candy or anything, but I think she liked the idea of having a boyfriend more than she liked me personally."

After seeing how quickly she hooked up with Chase, I'd come to the same conclusion. Maybe she'd just been afraid not to have someone.

"Why did you go with her for so long, if you didn't want to be her boyfriend?"

"It wasn't that I didn't *want* to be her boyfriend. Just never really planned to be."

"Chase is her boyfriend now," I said.

"Yeah, I heard. There aren't many secrets on this island."

Leaning back, I nestled my head into the nook of his shoulder.

"The heater's not running," he said quietly. "We should probably go downstairs where you've got the fire going in the fireplace."

"Probably. Or we could get the blankets off the bed."

But we didn't do either. I could hear the candle crackling. It was romantic.

"So you've dated a lot," he said. "What did the guys say when they asked you out?"

"They all said different things. You should say your words, not theirs."

"But the first time I ask a girl out, if she says no, I might be scarred for life."

His voice held a hint of teasing. But I thought maybe he was really nervous. As nervous as I was about where we might be heading.

"Why would she say no?" I asked.

"Why would she say yes? She's been avoiding me lately."

"You'll never know her answer unless you ask."

He kissed the soft spot just below my ear. It tickled and I curled my shoulder inward, which brought my mouth closer to his.

And then he was kissing me. It was so wonderful.

He pressed his palm against my cheek, turning my face for a better angle. I shifted around until I was sitting across his lap. I burrowed more closely against him so his jacket almost formed a cocoon around me.

He deepened the kiss. A little dab. A lot of swirl.

Drawing back slightly, he said, "Will you go out

with me tomorrow night?"

"Oh, yeah," I said, nodding quickly. "Oh, yeah."

And then he was kissing me again.

22

For our first date, we didn't exactly "go out." Technically, we were snowed in.

The storm had continued through the night. Eventually we moved down to the parlor so we could snuggle on the couch in front of the fire with several blankets tucked in around us.

And we talked. About everything and nothing. What school on the island was like, with all the grades in one building, the lilac festival, the fudgies, what it was like to be the rock-skipping champ, our favorites on everything . . . And we ended and started each new topic with a kiss. I didn't think I'd ever kissed any of my dates as much as I kissed Josh.

But then, I hadn't wanted to.

Being with Josh was so different from being with any other guy I'd ever dated. It was more than the fact that we had so much in common. I just liked being with him. I liked looking at him. I enjoyed talking with him. I wanted to know what he thought about things. And I wanted to share what I thought.

And the kissing. Oh my gosh, the kissing. My feet were in danger of cramping because my toes were curling so much, but I didn't care. Cramp, cramp away. It was worth it to kiss Josh.

He served me breakfast—another grilled cheese sandwich—in bed. Or I should say breakfast in couch, since the parlor was the warmest room in the house, and it was where I planned to stay for the duration of the storm.

I fixed him lunch.

And we made supper together.

Even though the electricity had come back on by then, we still ate by candlelight. But at least we could eat in the kitchen because the heater was running again.

We'd just settled on the couch to watch a horror movie—with a bowl of buttery popcorn between us—when Josh's cell phone rang. He looked at it. "My dad."

He answered. "Hey, Dad . . . no, I'm fine. After you called last night, I, uh, I actually came over to Ashleigh's to make sure she was okay and the weather was so bad that I ended up staying." He grimaced. "Yes, sir, I know. I behaved." He rolled his eyes. "When will you be back?" He mouthed, "Tomorrow" and then said, "That's what I figured. Snow has us packed in, so I'll dig us out tomorrow." He winked at me.

We'd been talking about staying snowed in through the winter. And that was such a strange thing for me, to want to spend that much time with a guy. I usually got bored so quickly, was ready to move on so soon. Everything was different with Josh. It was comfortable, but scary. And I didn't know how it could be both, but it was.

I wondered if Tara was going to be surprised when I finally called her, or if she'd known all along that I'd feel this way if I gave Josh a chance.

"Your mom wants to talk to you," Josh said, handing me the phone.

"Hey, Mom."

"Ashleigh, Josh's dad told me that Josh is there with you. Are you okay?"

"I'm fine, Mom."

"I expect you two to behave yourselves."

"We will. I promise."

"I wish we could get back today."

"Don't worry, Mom. We'll be okay, and you can trust me."

"I know I can," Mom said. "Hopefully, we'll see

you tomorrow. I love you."

"I love you, too."

I handed the phone back to Josh and he talked to his dad a little longer. Then he hung up and picked up the remote.

"You ready?" he asked.

It was a horror movie I'd never seen. Before he'd headed over here, he'd stuffed it into his jacket pocket just in case we got snowed in and needed something to watch. I liked a guy who came prepared.

"I'm ready," I said.

"I'm gonna be watching you."

"Why watch me? Watch the movie."

"I need proof that you watch horror movies with your eyes wide open."

"Proof? Why would you need proof?"

"Because my first girlfriend was a girly-girl when we watched horror. I don't want my next girlfriend to be."

My heart thumped in my chest—thumped from excitement, not fear. I snuggled up against him, reached for the remote, and punched play.

I didn't close my eyes once.

It was almost a week before we had our official first date. Mom and Mr. Wynter had finally returned to the island, well and happy. With lots of new wallpaper.

Mom didn't seem surprised that I had a date. She seemed really glad. Turns out my attitude about never having a boyfriend worried her. Here I'd thought Tara was weird for hooking up with Shaun of the Dead, and Mom had thought I was weird for not hooking up with anyone.

"I knew it! I knew it!" Tara had shouted when I'd finally told her that Josh and I were going on an official date. And she immediately started talking about all the things that the four of us would do when she and Shaun came back to the island in the summer.

"I can't confirm," I told her. "I can't think that far ahead."

"Okay, okay, but just consider it a possibility that you'll still be with him come summer."

Squeezing my eyes shut, I took a deep breath. "Okay."

We might still be dating then. If I survived tonight.

I was nervous. I didn't know what to expect. Josh hadn't told me anything, except to dress warmly.

I went with my usual jeans tucked into boots. I was wearing an emerald green cowl-necked sweater. It was really soft. I didn't think it would keep me terribly warm, but I just couldn't go the whole bundled-up-like-an-Eskimo route. I wanted to look a little sexy. Okay, I wanted to look a lot sexy. I wanted Josh to be amazed.

Strange that after spending so much time together during the last week, we were still learning so much about each other. And I loved every minute that I discovered something new about him.

I was pacing in the parlor when I heard the sleigh bells.

I pulled back the curtain and looked outside. Josh was climbing out of a sleigh.

I wanted to believe it was because he was a romantic, but I knew he saw it as just a mode of travel. So now I was left to wonder where we were going.

Mom was looking over my shoulder. "Isn't that sweet?"

I didn't want to disappoint Mom the romantic, so I just said, "Very."

I gave her a big hug and was out the door before Josh got to the porch.

"You ready?" he asked.

"Oh, yeah. I can't believe you hired a sleigh."

"Someone I know told me that chicks think

sleigh rides are romantic. And if I'm only going to get a couple of dates, I want to make them count."

"What makes you think you're going to get only a couple?" I asked.

"How many do you think I'm good for?"

I studied him, then gave him a big smile. "Definitely more than a couple." Probably a hundred. A thousand even.

He helped me climb into the sleigh, behind the driver, who was sitting on a seat in front of us. Josh got in and tucked a blanket around our laps and our legs.

He told the driver we were ready. The driver slapped the reins and the horses took off.

"So where are we going?" I asked.

"Just around the island for a while, then we'll go to V.P. and grab something to eat. And there's a movie showing at one of the smaller hotels that I thought we'd catch."

"Sounds like fun."

"You know what I figured out during the last week?" he asked.

"What?"

"Snow and winter, they go together."

I snuggled more closely against him. "Yeah, we do."

Sneaux and Wynter—we definitely go together.

"I need to ask you something," he said.

He sounded so serious. It made me nervous. I moved back slightly and studied him. For the first time in days, I couldn't read his thoughts. "Okay. Go ahead."

He reached into his pocket and pulled out a small sheet of paper and a tiny flashlight. As I unfolded the paper, he shone the flashlight on it.

WILL YOU BE MY GIRLFRIEND? CHECK YES OR NO.

[] YES   [] NO

I laughed. "Is this really the way you want to do it?"

"It'll leave no doubts. I'll know exactly where I stand. And if you check no, it's okay. I know you don't want a boyfriend, and I can respect that. But that doesn't mean I won't keep asking or hoping to change your mind. Especially if I get some bonus dates."

"I don't have a pen."

He did. He handed it to me.

I checked the box. Then I threw my arms around his neck and kissed him.

Because I had, of course, checked yes.

The best winter vacation, the best new friend,
the best romance . . .

The Best Girl

"Jane?" Biff repeated, confused.

I shot her a silencing look that I could only hope she would understand, and unfolded myself from the floor. Connor reached out and took my arm and hoisted me up. My already pounding heart went spastic. Hot Connor had just touched me. Was still touching me, actually. His hand was clasped around my forearm as he stared at me in unadulterated shock.

"Wh . . . what are you doing here?" I stammered.

"I work here," he said. That much was obvious. Not only was he in the kitchen in the middle of the night, but he was wearing a full suit and tie under his puffy River Lodge down parka, and his normally sexy-stubble-covered face was perfectly clean-shaven. And still gorgeous, of course. "What are *you* doing here?"

Behind me, Biff stood up, kicking the cake box back under the butcher's block and out of sight.

"Oh, we were just . . . we got lost. I mean, this place is huge and I took a . . . a wrong turn and I—"

Connor laughed. It was a nice laugh. "No, I don't mean here in the kitchen. Even though I am curious. I mean here at the lodge."

"Oh." Duh, Farrah. "I'm here for a wedding."

Instantly something in his face shifted. He released his grip on my arm and I felt a sudden chill.

"You're kidding," he said. "You're with them?"

Biff and I exchanged a look. That had not been a good tone.

"Them who?" Biff asked.

Connor looked at both of us and I could practically see his brain working, realizing he'd already said too much. "Nothing. Forget it," he said, waving a hand and turning away. "You guys really shouldn't be back here. You should probably—"

"No, really. What were you going to say?" Biff prodded, leaning into one of the counter-tops. "Because if you're talking about all the overprivileged snobs running around this place like they own it, we're not *with* them."

"You're not?" Connor asked doubtfully.

Biff looked at me and pursed her lips, trying to get me to back her up.

"Uh, no. No. We're not," I put in, feeling lame.

"But if you're here for the wedding . . ."

"Yeah, we're nannies," Biff said. "For the Janssen family? The groom has these two little brothers. We take care of them."

"Seriously?" Connor asked. He was clearly pleased by this news. He looked to me for confirmation. "You're a nanny."

"Girl's gotta make a living somehow," I improvised.

More fun and flirting from Rachel Hawthorne!

The Boyfriend League
Dani's a tomboy, totally useless when it comes to romance. Can she and her best friend change her luck when both of their families host a whole summer league of potential boyfriends?

First Kisses 1: Trust Me
Jess plans to be the best camp counselor ever until she finds out that her partner for trust-training is the untrustworthy Sean Reed. But will Jess fall in love with him anyway?

Thrill Ride
Megan Holloway has found the perfect summer job. But can Megan and her dreamy new boyfriend survive a long-distance relationship ...and her incredibly hot coworker?

Love on the Lifts
Kate Kennedy and her friends figure out a way to get warm on the slopes after her brother and his cute friends show up. But will her obsession with super-hot Brad interfere with her chance of true love?

Island Girls (And Boys)
Three best friends, one beach house...plus a stray dog, a cat, and a live-in boyfriend. It's not exactly the summer Jennifer was expecting. But then again, she also wasn't expecting to fall in love.

Caribbean Cruising
Lindsay decides that her cruise will be the perfect place to begin her "summer of firsts." But she soon discovers that it is impossible to have a fling—when you're actually falling in love.